MARRIAGE ISN'T ALWAYS
A BED OF ROSES ...

"Kenny, you need to calm down so we can talk about this rationally."

His fist came down like thunder on the mantelpiece, rattling everything on it. "How long, Maxine, were you going to play me for a fool? Huh? How long were you and the 'professor' there going to act like you were in class every Wednesday night!"

"Oh, now see, you have just gone too far, Kenneth Chadway." This man had lost his damned mind, accusing her like that. "So now I'm running around, all because you saw me having a cup of coffee with my teacher in a diner? Oh, like if I were having an affair, I'd tell you where I'd be, and be there? That just makes all the sense in the world." Maxine paced as her ire gained momentum. "Like you didn't want a chance to explain when *you* were in a shaky predicament that wasn't your fault?"

She knew she had him when he looked away and mumbled, "That was different."

Based upon the television series *Soul Food*
Developed for television by Felicia D. Henderson
Based upon characters created for the motion picture *Soul Food*
Written by George Tillman, Jr.

soul food
the series

THROUGH THICK AND THIN

Leslie Esdaile

writing as
Leslie E. Banks

POCKET STAR BOOKS
New York London Toronto Sydney Singapore

This book is a work of fiction. Names, characters, places and incidents are products of the author's imagination or are used fictitiously. Any resemblance to actual events or locales or persons, living or dead, is entirely coincidental.

An *Original* Publication of POCKET BOOKS

 A Pocket Star Book published by
POCKET BOOKS, a division of Simon & Schuster, Inc.
1230 Avenue of the Americas, New York, NY 10020

ISBN: 0-7434-6292-0

First Pocket Books printing March 2003

10 9 8 7 6 5 4 3 2 1

POCKET STAR BOOKS and colophon are registered trademarks of Simon & Schuster, Inc.

For information regarding special discounts for bulk purchases, please contact Simon & Schuster Special Sales at 1-800-456-6798 or business@simonandschuster.com

Cover photo by Matthew Jordan Smith

Printed in the U.S.A.

THROUGH THICK AND THIN

one

Maxine Chadway stood in front of the kitchen sink, allowing the faucet to drizzle cool water over her partially frozen pork chops as she separated them for dinner. She'd have to break the news to her husband tonight. Kenny would have a fit about her wanting to take an evening writing class—not because he wasn't supportive, but the man hated change. Her being gone at night once a week would alter his routine.

But hadn't there been many warning signs that it was indeed time for a change? Her sister, Bird, had just narrowly missed ovarian cancer—and Bird's household had to adapt, just as the whole family did when some of them narrowly escaped being killed in a car accident. God had been good to her loved ones, and to her, and she wasn't trying to tempt fate. So many families hadn't been as lucky on September 11. . . . All she'd been able to focus on since then, trying to tuck worries about her own children into the recesses of her mind, was, What if something happened to her? Who would tell her children about their rich family history, its roots?

Sure, her sisters might fill in the gaps, as would Kenny and Bird's husband, Lem. But it wasn't the same as hearing it from their mother. She looked down at the pork chops in her hands, trying to remember how *her* mother used to season them. There were so many things she'd wanted to ask Mama Joe, but time had passed by, and now the opportunity was gone, just like her mother was.

And that's why she couldn't continue to put off her dreams for tomorrow. She would follow through with this one; nothing would stand in her way. You just never knew how much time you had, and you couldn't take the gift of life for granted.

She'd lived with Kenny and loved him long enough to know that, as long as his daily pattern wasn't greatly compromised, he wouldn't have a problem with her wanting to try something new. Why couldn't this class have been held during the day while the bigger kids were in school, and a baby-sitter for a couple of hours would be easier to find for her little one?

But now, for six weeks, the entire household routine would be in chaos, and there would be no way that Kenny's world order would remain untouched. Maxine sighed. She did not feel like having a verbal heavyweight boxing match with him about this tonight. She wanted to write, and to learn from one of the best in a community-sponsored class. Was that so much to ask?

She glanced at her reheated greens from Sunday to see how they were advancing, and checked the moisture level in the pot of rice. Kenny would be home soon. The children were all accounted for, the older two occupied with homework and laying out their clothes for the next morning, and her baby girl happily engrossed in a Fisher-Price toy for the moment. All she needed was a few minutes to get dinner on, and then she could make the rounds to check each child's homework progress. The conversation with Kenny would be delicate; so she'd ease into it slowly, gracefully, and pray that he'd for once just concede.

Her gaze floated out the window. March had indeed come in like a lion, wind whipping the backyard hedges, scattering swirls of leaves, and making the kitchen panes rattle. There was so much to do. Was dreaming just a waste of precious energy? Soon it would be time for spring cleaning: washing the curtains in here and switching over the closets. Easter was on the way, too—which meant she'd have to assess who had what in their closets, and do a wardrobe buy all around. Shoes, for sure; all the kids' feet were sprouting like weeds. How was she going to squeeze in writing?

Tonight she'd have to throw in two more loads of laundry, since she'd only gotten four done today—the heavy stuff, towels and bed linens. She'd gone to the library, and then come home inspired and wasted time writing.

Ahmad's hamper was overflowing, as usual. Kenny needed uniforms—his work duds were filthy. Kelly was getting to the finicky stage of wanting to always dress herself, and thus needed plenty of options. That child was so indecisive. Her sweet pea was the easiest one in the bunch but, as the baby, went through changes like crazy. Maxine sighed again. What had she been thinking when she'd procrastinated on dealing with the inevitable?

The phone rang, but she didn't bother to answer it. By inexplicable instinct, she could always tell when it was Kenny or one of her sisters on the line. However, with a teenaged son in the house, the telephone didn't stand a chance. Ahmad always raced for it as though the state lottery board was calling him with a winning ticket number.

Maxine waited a moment, and when she didn't hear "Mom!" yelled, she smiled, patting a chop dry on a paper towel and repeating the process with another piece of meat. At least her son was old enough now to know how to screen telemarketers. She'd give the boy ten minutes, then pick up and hang up without listening—the signal for him to stop breathing in some girl's ear and to get back to his homework.

A chuckle found its way to her throat. She'd just been working on a short poem earlier about that very thing. God, she remembered those days—running for the phone, hoping it was Kenny, and battling with her sisters for that one black rotary unit that sat in the center of the living room.

Her musing kept her company as she stood before the sink, her hands moving and her brain unlocking new prose. Kids didn't know how lucky they had it these days. There was no such thing as a cordless phone that allowed for private conversations. No TV in anybody's room, or computers to help correct spelling errors on reports. Hell, her son would faint if she gave him that old IBM Selectric still in the basement, the one that had once been considered modern technology and that required skill and dexterity to use—lining up the paper just so, making sure you put the carbon paper between two clean sheets in it, purple all over your fingers if you wanted a copy . . . corrector tape.

And chores! Maxine laughed out loud, thinking back on how there was no such thing as no-wax floors. Baseboards were done by hand. Dusting meant this oily stuff that went on a rag, not some easy, magnetic spray that practically picked up the dust for you as you swiped a cloth by it. Vacuum cleaners were as heavy as a Sherman tank, not plastic, easy-glide contraptions that took only a few minutes to push across a floor. They didn't know what housework and Saturdays meant for the Joseph girls. Nosiree, they didn't. Oh, yeah, she had to add that bit of historical wisdom into the poem—or maybe it would be a short story?

Supermarket shopping was a process then, too. Yeah. She remembered it like it was yesterday. There was the butcher, the fish man, the vegetable man, and then Mama Joe went to the store. Humph. Her mother did all the baking, so there was no buying cupcakes and Twinkies, and juice boxes for lunch. When lunch went to school, it was in a *real* brown bag, or a metal lunch box. During winters, you carried a huge thermos with mirrored glass inside it, filled with homemade soup, that you'd better not drop, lest it shatter and Mama would whip your butt for the waste.

Her kids had no concept. Back then nothing was disposable, nothing was throwaway. . . . People weren't, either. Her Chadway crew had light duty. They shoulda been in Mama Joe's Marine Corps! Microwaves, plastic, Ziploc baggies—everything was so easy these days. Yup. She'd go back in time and tell her story from her mama's house. Her poem would be a short story.

But some things *hadn't* changed since the beginning of time. Another sigh pushed its way past Maxine's lips. Teenagers still ran for the phone. She tried to jettison the warm but melancholy memory of her mother from her mind as she sprayed the large Pyrex baking dish with low-fat cooking oil and arranged the dried chops within it. Baked was better, healthier. Her husband didn't need to be eating all that old-fashioned food—no matter what he fussed about. Fried, smothered pork chops would shorten his life. Simple knowledge like that might have saved, or at least added years to, her mother's life. But back then, who knew? Even the food charts were changing—and her husband hated change. Yet some change was good.

Maxine glanced at the running market list held up by a magnet on the refrigerator. More chicken and fish, regardless of what Kenny said. She loved him, and he was gonna be healthy or bust. *That* she would fight with him about—she wasn't taking any prisoners on that issue. Why, Lord, was everything always such a struggle with this man? The pork chops were his weekly meat quotient, but who knew what he snuck in at work? Burgers, for sure, even though she'd packed him a healthy lunch.

All she could hope was that he'd be too busy during the day, or too frugal, to stop for fast food when good food was within his grasp. She needed to add lean ground turkey to her list, too, along with more fresh vegetables and paper towels. God spare the trees, because her family had probably gone through a forest on its own. Wasting paper towels was bad on the environment, but they just snatched a towel down from the dispenser, blotted up the tiniest mess, and then tossed it. Maxine stopped moving for a moment.

Truth be told, she'd wasted her share of paper today, crumpling up page after page of typing paper. What had she been thinking when she'd used the baby's naptime messing around on Ahmad's computer? Tonight she'd pay for the hour and a half she'd spent trying to collect and compose her thoughts. Prose just didn't come during the day. Nights were when her creativity flowed, but that was next to impossible. Once the kids got settled and she'd cried uncle to the unending list of chores, then it was Kenny's time.

Maxine blinked back sudden, inexplicable tears and started moving again like a speed demon. What was wrong with her? There was nothing to cry about, certainly nothing as crazy as this mess. A deep breath steadied her as she worked.

All of this was ridiculous. She knew she couldn't use Ahmad's computer at night—he needed it for his homework, or would be playing video games, or chatting on-line with his friends. Besides, she could barely think in his cluttered room when he wasn't in it, let alone if he were popping in and out and sweating her about when she'd be finished. Real truth be told, she needed her own little laptop—something small and unobtrusive that she could open up on the kitchen table late at night when none of the family needed her, where she could go off into her own world and simply think, or be, or create. The old IBM typewriter was cumbersome and didn't correct mistakes easily, and the click-clack of the ball hitting the paper would assuredly drive her husband nuts at night—and she'd hear about it. The man worked hard and needed his rest, and a laptop would be a good compromise.

But the expense was out of the question, especially when there was already one computer in the house. Still . . . She could hear Kenny's protest in her head before the thought even formed. "Maxine, you know I just got this new city towing contract and have to reinvest in the business that pays the household bills. We have to tighten our belts and put hard-earned money into things that last—like the children's education, the house, the business, not foolishness. And not a hobby."

Guilt congealed with a tinge of anger—that's why she needed her own source of capital, so she didn't always have to *ask* for everything. If she had just a little income of her own, she could do a few things that were not on the Kenny-waiver list. Not that he denied her anything, really. But what did she actually ask for? Her requests were always for the family: the kids needed shoes, Kelly needed a coat, Ahmad needed books or new sports gear, the baby needed a bigger snowsuit, the windows needed new frames, the storm door needed a new hinge. Maintenance. She was not on that list.

Maxine looked at her hands and down at her sweatpants and T-shirt. She didn't waste money on nails. She didn't waste money, period. Her hair was all natural, and her sister, Bird, kept her locks looking good for free. It was good to have a salon owner in the family, just like it was good to have a lawyer sister, and a husband and brother-in-law who could fix just about anything that broke. She didn't buy makeup or clothes— God only knew the last time she'd bought something new for herself. Since she only went to school functions for the kids and to church, there hadn't been a need to buy clothes. Where did she go these days that warranted getting dressed up in the latest fashions?

"Not that I'm complaining, Lord. You know that. I'm just being realistic about what has to be done," she murmured, closing her eyes as she asked for forgiveness. "I am blessed. I am well provided for. Wants are pure vanity."

She washed her hands and went to her spice rack to select what she needed to season the meat. The chops should have been thawed earlier and already prepped to allow the flavor to get through them, especially since she was baking them. But she'd wasted time trying to write junk. She clicked the burner off under her rice and grabbed a fork, whipping the moist grains around to let the residual heat from the burner finish the process. The greens were ready, too, and would stay hot if she kept the lid on them. Forty minutes, and the chops would be ready to come out. Cornbread took fifteen minutes from out of the box to the table. Oh, well, her family knew better than to expect homemade during the week. Thank God for some inventions.

During the week—Maxine stopped and held the pan of meat in midair. It was Wednesday night. Tomorrow Kelly needed brownies for the school fund-raiser. Ahmad had a class trip, and had to be to school earlier than usual—so she had to drive him, which meant everybody had to leave earlier with her. Plus, tonight was *Wednesday* night . . . Kenny's midweek night. Like a *Saturday* night. Shit.

She flung the chops in the oven, went into the living

room, spied the table, and took a deep breath. "Kelly, Ahmad, set the table!"

A series of okays echoed back through the house.

"Not later. Now, guys!"

Laundry had to go in immediately. *Wednesday night.* Her husband didn't ask for much. She glanced over her shoulder as she passed the playpen. Her baby was standing and reaching for her. "Mommy will be back in a second." Wails of discontent followed behind her. *Just a few minutes to do what I gotta do, Lord.*

She hurdled the stairs two at a time. The kids had to go to bed early; Ahmad had to get up extra early for the class trip. She should have gone to the store to put some extra goodies in the house to go with his super lunch, the lunch good moms were supposed to make for a kid to take on a bus trip. Permission slip—did she sign that already? Damn.

The baby was crying.

"Kelly, get your sister for me—I have to throw in some clothes!"

Maxine tore from room to room, toting a heavy basket in both arms and nearly bumping into Ahmad in the hall as she bustled toward his bedroom door.

"Dump me out your colored clothes," she ordered. "I'll throw in the whites in a few minutes once the first cycle is done."

Her son stood there looking at her with a stricken expression.

"You changed my bed," he muttered.

"Yeah, I did. Now listen—set the table, but first dump out the colored clothes—your uniform stuff."

Again no motion, and he still had the phone clutched

to his chest. She could feel her pulse beat in her temples. "Boy, what is wrong with you? Get off that dag-gonned phone and do as I say!"

"You don't have to change my bed, Mom. I'll do my own laundry."

Jesus help her, she was going to wring this child's neck if he didn't stop pushing her buttons. She didn't have time for this mess; tonight was parent night. Shoot! When he just stared at her, Maxine narrowed her gaze to convey a lethal warning. "I'm in no mood to debate with you right now."

She spun on her heels and went to Kelly's room. Damned kids just don't know—one day it'll be his turn to work all day like a Georgia mule and want a little private affection from his wife, and some teenager will be standing in the floor with an attitude. The mother's curse prevails—that boy just doesn't know! Heaven help her if that boy was still on the telephone and hadn't moved by the time she got back to his room. . . . Lord, stay her hand.

In three deft moves, she had set down the basket, collected Kelly's clothes, and was back in the hall. This was two loads right here, even without Ahmad's stuff, and she hadn't even begun to deal with the whites. Entering his room, using a foot to push open the semi-closed door, she dropped the basket on Ahmad's bed. Her son was moving like molasses in January, extracting dirty laundry item by item to drop it on the floor.

No patience left in her, she brushed past him, dug both hands in his hamper, and came away with an armload.

"Mom, don't!"

"Boy, I don't have time for your dawdling. Your father will be home soon and will want to eat; I have dinner on, and other things to do. Now what is all the hullabaloo about!"

Disgusted, she flung colored items into the waiting basket like she was an assembly-line speed sorter, ignoring her son's appalled expression. When she got to a crusty pair of gym shorts, Ahmad lunged for them, almost bumping their heads.

"I got it, I got it," he blurted out, seeming as though he'd lost his breath in a race.

Maxine stilled herself and looked at her child's stricken expression. Ahmad looked like he was about to faint dead away from embarrassment. Her shoulders slumped. Oh, right . . . she had a teenager in the house. *A son.* Lord have mercy. She softened her countenance and put her hands on her hips to preserve the boy's dignity. Her facial expression didn't change as she gave him the old "Mom is blind in one eye and can't see out of the other" routine.

"Listen, I don't have time for this, and I've been telling you to sort your laundry since Saturday. Now, I'm gonna go get the table ready, because I can smell my chops need turning. This is too heavy for me, anyway, so do me a favor and get the rest of the colored clothes in the basket and just take it all down the basement."

Her mortified child's shoulders dropped two inches, and he quickly bobbed his head in assent.

"Yeah, Mom, I got it—no need for you to do it, okay? I got it. Shoulda had it done, like you said. Okay? I can put them in the washer for you, too, Mom. No problem. Okay?"

"Ummm-hmmm," Maxine grumbled, leaving a relieved Ahmad to finish what she'd started. "And get off the telephone!" she called over her shoulder, heading downstairs with purpose.

Although the baby's wailing had ceased, it had been replaced by fussing. Every time Kelly put a napkin down, her baby sister squealed with the delight of snatching it from the table. The more Kelly fussed, the more the baby laughed at the game.

"Mom! I can't set the table. I'm trying, but she keeps pulling the stuff off."

Maxine stared at the once-clean forks that were on the floor, and blanched at the knives scattered at her feet.

"Girl, what is wrong with you? Why did you let her out of the playpen when you had knives on the table that she could reach?"

Without listening to the plaintive reply about how the baby refused to stay put, Maxine bent, began picking up silverware, and scooped up the toddler, who was shredding a paper napkin.

With a kiss she dumped her daughter, sans napkin, back in the holding pen and marched to the kitchen to turn the chops and rewash the knives and forks. If her husband had any idea what went on around the house during the day, and what it took to bring calm before he graced them with his presence . . . and he wanted a showered, rested, and amorous wife on a Wednesday night? Was the man on drugs, or something?

She opened the oven, turned the meat that had browned on one side, and glanced at the clock. Multitasking, she quickly washed the flatware, dumped it on a dishtowel to come back to shortly, and began making lunches as the baby squealed in a high pitch from the other room. She knew it wasn't politically correct, but cartoons were a lifesaver. Before Kelly even grabbed the iced tea, Maxine knew it was going to fall. Mother telepathy kicked in, and she steadied the child's efforts, avoiding a mop job as Kelly wobbled back through the kitchen doorway. Oh, yeah, this was rush hour—Kenny thought he drove his tow truck through rush hour; she *lived* in the zone. She had more mileage under her belt than on any radials in his garage.

Thirty minutes ticked away as lunches were made, laundry got started, Kelly's attempt to set the table was completed, and the littlest one was in a high chair with Cheerios to play with. Her son's dignity had been preserved. Ahmad was put on notice to deal with the white load—he'd wash them, she'd put them in the dryer. Her son had looked so relieved that she'd had to turn away to hide the smile. Been there, brother, she almost wanted to say to him. Like your father and I were born yesterday? Humph. That was a discussion for Kenny to have with his son.

All the homework was done; education in the Chadway residence was in full effect. Checkpoint down, a few more to go before Dad walked in the door. The littlest needed a bath, and she prayed the hot water would hold out with laundry simultaneously draining the tank. Damn, she should have done it earlier in the day!

Okay, it was about regrouping and picking up the lost time. Bedtime for baby bird, the youngest, would be seven-thirty. Then Kelly at eight o'clock. Ahmad had been told lights out by ten, and she knew he wouldn't argue tonight; he could barely look her in the eye. Fine. But first dinner, then kitchen KP. Dry the wet clothes, fold and stack them, and bring piles of them to the rooms . . . except Ahmad's. She didn't walk in his door without knocking anymore; she'd just yell through it to alert him that a clean clothing shipment was on the way. Teenagers.

Nine o'clock would see her on the sofa, sitting, for that one point in the week when she could—if she planned it right. An hour to listen to Kenny recount his day. And her divorced or still single girlfriends wondered why she no longer had time to talk or hang out, or do lunch! The old ladies from the church wondered why she was always stopping by and running errands with her car motor still running! Shoot, she barely had time to connect with her sisters. Sunday was when she could at least eat with them and put her eye on them.

Geez Louise. *The other mothers knew.*

Ten o'clock; lights out for the oldest. Ahmad would get over it. Then she and Kenny could watch the news and chat some more, to be sure all the kids were asleep. One hour to be sure there was a safety seal on little ears. Eleven. The washing machine should have stopped by then, though the dryer might have to run half the night. Maybe she'd take a shower; maybe not. She'd suggest that Kenny do so. He would, and would also smile. It was Wednesday night.

Then again, if there was any hot water left, maybe she'd run him a bath with Epsom salts and wash his back—they could talk while he bathed, and she could kill two birds with one stone—talk and pay him attention at the same time. Maybe the hot bath would total him and make him just go to sleep, so she could crash and burn. Damn, she was exhausted. But if he was feeling amorous, that would only give her fifteen minutes to mentally decompress, put on a nightgown, and breathe. She knew the drill, and writing had messed up her routine. What had been on her mind!

Maxine pushed a stray lock behind her ear and glanced down at her sweatpants and T-shirt, which had every task of the day clinging to them. She'd have to work in a shower; she was disgusting herself. Though stuff like that never seemed to bother her husband. Yuck. Cavemen. Neolithic. She laughed, glad that she had one anyway. She closed her eyes and allowed her head to drop back for a moment to chase away the tension.

Without needing to open her eyes, she could feel the presence of a small person beside her.

"Mommy, what's so funny?"

All Maxine could do was shake her head. "Nothing, baby. Go make sure your sister is okay in her high chair."

"You tired, Mommy? 'Cause your eyes are closed."

"No, baby," she whispered. The question made her chuckle and swallow hard at the same time. Moisture crept to her eyes. "Mommy's just taking a power nap standing up."

"Can I do that, too?"

"Yeah," Maxine murmured, opening her eyes and bending to kiss Kelly's forehead. "All mommies learn how to do that—one day I'll teach you. It's a survival skill."

Her daughter giggled and raced away to do her big-girl task of watching her baby sister. Maxine looked at the child's retreating form and reminded herself of every blessing she had in her life: wonderful, healthy children; a good husband who was a great father and an excellent provider; a good family. In the grand scheme of things, her issues were minimal. Her family's happiness was essential.

There was no need to rock the boat and to be unappreciative of anything God had bestowed upon her. It was not important that Kenny understand this quest to write stuff. Creativity was for single women, or women wealthy enough to have their own help. She'd been tripping. Easter shoes, paying the mortgage, getting lunches made—things of substance were important.

She walked over to the oven and began turning the meat again, satisfied with its progress. She wasn't going out on a limb to cause a cosmic disruption to the order of things, like other women did—they needed to chill, if they had something good, solid, and substantial around them. Black women couldn't just pick up and do something self-absorbed when they had a family. Especially if they'd been blessed with a good man to be their husband. What had been on her mind, anyway? About to kick up some dust for no good reason, not that she could ever be some Pulitzer Prize–winning poet, anyway. If her mother were alive, what would she have said? *Maxine, family first.* Probably.

Maxine stood up and glanced at the motion beyond the window caused by the howling March wind. What *would* her mother have said?

"Did you ever feel like this, Ma?" she murmured so quietly that the words were more of a thought than a sentence.

Her hand idly stroked the pocket that contained a flyer from the Free Library within it. Poet laureate and playwright Paul Gotier would be in town on his annual trek to give back to the community by teaching a seminar for free. The writing class was only six weeks long. Six Wednesday nights. Six nights that she hadn't asked for permission to claim for herself, before she'd signed up. And even though she'd felt lucky at getting on the list, it might mean six weeks of arguments with Kenny—who would flip about her absence at home on *their night.* What would her mother have done?

The word *permission* sent a shard of resentment through her. She was a grown woman and still seemed to require a permission slip to go on a six-week field trip, just like her son needed one from her for his school junket tomorrow. What was wrong with this picture?

The awareness was disturbing. What hidden talents and gifts had her mother taken to the grave? What things had Mama Joe left undone, or maybe just shared as loving anointments to her family's growth, but never employed toward her own fulfillment?

Maxine bent to lift the Pyrex dish from the oven. She then reached for a canister on the draining board and took out a small handful of flour as she put the stove burner on low under the meat to begin making gravy. Little by little she allowed the flour to sift from her fist, using the other hand to keep moving a fork within the thickening sauce, the way she'd learned from her mother. She knew it was healthier for Kenny not to have pan-made gravy, with all the fat drippings in it, but alas, it was Wednesday night.

It was all in the touch, so ephemeral an art—timing, proportion, the balance of just enough of this and that—learned by watching. Just like her daughters would learn to sublimate their gifts from watching her do it, too. Just like they would pick men, by watching the way she interacted with the one she'd chosen—or more precisely, who'd chosen her. Maxine stirred the pan faster, not at all liking the direction her insane thoughts were going. She wiped her floury hand against her sweatpants. She was *completely* happy, dammit.

"Hey, Maxine! Smells good, baby!"

Tension pulled her spine to attention as she forced a smile and tilted her head, waiting for the sound of heavy boots to cross the living room and enter the kitchen. A kiss would land on her cheek in less than two minutes—by the time the gravy was done. She was on schedule, and the household train of complete order had not derailed.

"Hey, baby. How was your day?" She called back the question by rote, her voice rising in a pleasant lilt.

"Hawk is flying high, as usual. Cold as all get-out. What's cooking?"

Maxine just stared at her empty palm, still whitened by the flour, while her other hand kept a steady, unbroken rhythm.

two

Kenny rolled his neck and sank deeper into the tub with a satisfied groan. God, Maxine knew how to work a soapy sponge. He loved Wednesday nights. Looked forward to them all week. Plus, she'd fed him like a champ, put the kids to bed, and her hands were massaging the kinks out of his shoulders in a way that made it all worthwhile. What else could a man ask for?

Constant, circular motion from the sponge on one side of him competed with the sensation of her fingers as they gently tugged at his sore muscles.

"If you weren't sitting here on the edge of the tub, baby, I might fall asleep and drown, this feels so good." He closed his eyes, breathing in her fresh-showered scent and enjoying every moment of her attention to his weary body.

"How's your back?"

"Feels like someone loaded cinder blocks on it," he grunted, shifting to lean forward so she could reach his spine. Even her soft voice sounded like a gentle stroke on him. When she moved to begin lathering soap and applying attention to where his back hurt, her beige silk nightgown brushed his arm. He didn't open his eyes. Her flattened palms pushed against every aching cord that ran the length of his spine until she made him grunt again. Then she did what she always did—touched his scar from the surgery that he'd undergone after the car accident. Maxine's fingers glided over the keloided area as though adding a balm of reverence before she applied more direct pressure.

"Oh, yeah . . . right there, Maxine . . . ," he murmured, near delirium. That's also what he loved about her. She knew. She always knew. Could find any hurt and make it go away, inside his soul, or within his body.

"Did I tell you how much I love you?" he whispered as her hands began a firm, lathered sweep of his back.

"Every Wednesday night for years," she chuckled, kissing the nape of his neck while she continued to work on him. "Plus some Saturday nights. I love you, too."

"It is good, isn't it?" Oh, yeah, his wife made going out in the streets in the ass-biting cold worth it. To come home to this? Yeah. "Kids asleep, you think?"

"Give them some more time," she murmured near his ear, sending a warm shaft of air into it. "Besides, you haven't told me about your day yet."

She slid down the side of the tub so she could face him as she sat soaping his upper arms. Until she'd touched them, he hadn't realized just how much he'd used that part of his body all day. He could barely hold his head up, but he wanted to look at her pretty face. Even cocoa brown with a mischievous grin . . . thick, dark lashes, and eyes that still sparkled the way they did when they were in high school. He allowed his gaze to travel down the bridge of her nose to her lush lips, and over her breasts, which peeked at him through the sheer gown. The fabric was clinging to her from the damp heat in the bathroom, and the effect was mesmerizing. Although exhausted, he felt himself stir.

"What day?" he murmured with a grin.

"You need to let me work the kinks out of you before you start something and catch a cramp, brother."

They both laughed.

"The truth, Maxine. My mind is eighteen, but my body isn't anymore . . . although you do have a way of making me forget certain realities."

Her gentle hands found his chest. "You need to go easy on this body. Not try to do it all yourself."

He leaned up enough to brush her mouth with a brief kiss, then sat back again. "I do it all for you and the kids, and don't regret a minute of it . . . especially when you work on me like this afterward."

He loved the shy smile that she offered now. It always did something to him when she glanced away like that—sitting there all pretty, wearing that particular gown, watching beads of moisture form in her cleavage . . . he'd waited all day for this.

"How's your legs?" Her tone was lazy and sexy and low.

"Which one?" He chuckled, and then bent his knee to expose his thigh. He had to close his eyes as her finger firmly traced the soreness there. When her hands slid down his calf, he winced. Damn aging.

"Girl, they got blood from a stone today. I stopped counting tow jobs—and the wind was cutting like a razor out there. I can't complain, though. Every tow job means more for the business, more for us. So it's all good . . . but I'm beat."

"Uhmmm-hmmm. I can feel it in your legs."

Now, how was she supposed to bring the subject up? Maxine studied her husband's strong build and the way his bronze skin looked so appetizing while wet. The man had worked hard today, and all he wanted was a hot meal, some peace, and a little somethin' somethin'—which was a mutual benefit. Her plan to get this thing off her chest was backfiring as he stared at her.

Maybe it was working on his body, or the steam in the bathroom, but she could definitely feel heat against her skin making her resolve melt. She tried to focus. Kenny always had this effect on her; that's where their last baby came from.

"You look like you're a million miles away, Maxine. I never asked you how your day was, did I?"

"Oh, my day," she scoffed. "Same ole, same ole." What could she say? There were things she needed to tell him, fears and worries she had about the future, but she didn't want to burden him with all of that. Didn't really have the language to wrap around the sinking feeling of mortality. How did one articulate being afraid about everything in general and yet nothing in particular?

"That's good," he murmured, closing his eyes as her hand rubbed his torso.

She tensed. That was good? That her day was the same ole, same ole?

He opened his eyes.

"What's the matter?"

"Nothing," she said quickly, gathering herself together

as the heat she'd been feeling went cool within her.

"Something happened today, didn't it?" Kenny sat up and took the soapy sponge from her hands. "What did Ahmad do?"

"Oh, he didn't do anything," she said, trying to keep things light. "But you do need to talk to your son again." She issued Kenny a sly wink. "He's going through it. Insists on doing his own laundry these days."

Kenny laughed, and his body relaxed. "Yeah, I remember those days. Not much I can do to help the boy. It's a rite of passage. Don't worry, honey."

Maxine shook her head with a smile. The discussion could wait. Why rock the boat? He was in such a good mood.

"One day he'll get a beautiful wife, too. Then he won't have to worry about it."

She could feel her spine straighten despite her will to keep things on a peaceful track.

"He won't have to worry about his laundry then, is what you're saying?" The words had come from her lips before she could censor them.

"Yeah . . ." Kenny sighed, oblivious to the shift in mood temperature in the bathroom.

"He won't have to cook, or clean, or any of that mundane stuff either, then?"

Kenny opened his eyes and began rinsing the soap off him. "Honey, now, you know that's not what I meant. I meant he'd have a gorgeous wife like I do, God willing, and . . . What happened today? What did that boy do? Did he slack on his chores around here? I'll kill him if he upset you today. Seriously, what's on your mind?"

It was now or never.

"I saw a flyer in the library for a writing class, and—"

"—well, baby, you know I'd support you, if that's what you want to do."

She swallowed a smile, trying to keep her eyes on his and not his erection. Yeah, he'd be supportive, while naked, in the bathroom, with a Wednesday-night hard-on. This was not how the discussion was supposed to go.

"Kenny," she said with a resigned sigh, "it's a six-week class." This wasn't some little one-hour day-seminar. It was a real class, taught by *Paul Gotier*. This was a commitment to her craft, and she'd have homework, and would need to really polish her projects to fully contribute and get the most out of the experience. It would mean that he might have to pick up some of the slack around the house.

"Well, Maxine, that's a good thing," he said carefully, seeming to consider her and her words. "A class. That's positive."

She was biting the insides of her cheeks to keep from grinning too much. Kenny's gaze was so furtive, and it was obvious that he was trying too hard to squash this discussion fast—he was looking forward to tonight more than she'd imagined. Flattered that he wanted her so much, still she pressed on. She wanted him, too—but that wasn't the point. She needed him to understand, and not just give lip service to her request because it was Wednesday and he was horny.

"But, Kenny . . . it's an *evening* class."

Silence.

She knew it.

She stood up and began washing the soap off her hands at the sink.

"Uh, Maxine, which night of the week?" He stood, grabbed a towel, and wrapped it around his waist.

"Wednesdays."

There. She'd said it.

"For how long?"

"Six weeks."

He stepped out of the tub and flipped the drain latch to let the water out.

"Six weeks, huh?"

"Yup."

"It has to be on a Wednesday night?"

"That's when they are offering the seminar."

"Oh."

"What does that mean?" Her hands had somehow found her hips.

"Just, oh. Like, oh, I didn't know."

"Oh," she grumbled.

"Don't get angry, Maxine. Oh, just meant, oh . . . like I'll miss the hell out of our Wednesday nights." He smiled at her.

How was she supposed to keep a sense of righteous indignation with him dripping wet, and his eyes seeming like they were eating her alive? She was already missing her Wednesday nights with him, and she hadn't even begun to take the class. Was she insane? But she had to know that he would support her interests as much as she'd been there to support his. This was important. It was about respect for her dreams.

"Kenny, this is a real commitment. I may have

assignments, and stuff to do—I'm not really sure what it will entail, except that I'll be there on Wednesday nights. You could have said more than 'Oh.' What does 'Oh' mean?"

He took a step closer. "Oh, like, I'm going to have to put a firm down payment on this Wednesday night to make up for the ones I'll be missing." He took another step nearer. "Like, oh, my God, I hope my wife is not asking me to give up our midweek rendezvous?"

"Oh, no. Definitely not," she said fast, taking a step closer to him and finding it impossible not to smile. "Tuesday, Thursday, any night would be fine."

"Oh." He cocked his head to the side and offered a jaunty expression.

She laughed. He joined her with a deep chuckle from inside his chest.

"Oh doesn't sound so bad, now does it—when you put it in context?"

"No, it doesn't," she whispered, her hands finding the center of his chest. "I can leave dinner ready to heat up, and I'll make arrangements for someone to be here with the children for a couple of hours until you come home."

"You'll take the cell phone, and let me know you got there safely, and when you leave—while you're in your car, you'll call—so I know you'll get back all right?"

"I promise." He had no idea how much that meant to her, that he wanted her to be safe, and was giving her his blessing without a fight. Her body relaxed, and a new desire for him began to smolder. Tonight she'd show him just how much she appreciated his simple, but very important, words.

His hands found her waist and slid down her backside, sending a shiver of anticipation with them.

"Oh . . . ," she sighed.

"You think the kids are asleep yet?"

"Want me to check on them?"

"No."

They both laughed a quiet, private laugh before he kissed her.

"I just wanted your full support, Kenny. This writing thing in me just won't go away." Her eyes searched his face for understanding. "After seeing all that we've seen, and all the chaos of the present, I want to write things down for the family, for our kids. You know, chronicle what it was like in our era and make some comparisons so there's a written legacy for our children to look back on." She sighed and touched his cheek. "Am I making any sense?"

His finger traced her jawline. "Baby, you can do that without going to a class, and you have all the time in the world to pick away at your personal project. But if you're dead set on going to a class, you know I've always supported any crazy schemes you've come up with. I love you. If you want to dabble in a new hobby, then—"

"Crazy schemes? A hobby?" She pulled away from him in disbelief and stood there numb, frustration and anger commingling to create a different kind of flame—one in her soul named rage.

Oh shit, he'd done it now, Kenny thought. But what did he say? They'd laughed together before about her wild concepts. Please, not tonight. Not on *this* night. Kenny stared at his wife; the sparkle was gone from her eyes, replaced by a blaze he k̲... *say wrong? Not tonight.*

"Baby—"

"How is running for councilperson a c... or a hobby? I almost won!"

"Yes, but—"

"And it wasn't crazy for me to help out at Chadway Towing when you got hurt, was it?"

"No, but—"

"And I still kept this house running like it was a navy ship. Am I right?"

"Maxine, baby, listen—"

"How is wanting to leave my own mark on the world a crazy scheme?"

She was out of the bathroom and pacing down the hall to their bedroom. Sudden tears of frustration were forming in her eyes, and she blinked them back. No. Not tonight. She wasn't going there. She knew her husband was from the turn of the century in how he viewed household roles. Most of the time she loved that about him. Tonight it was wearing a hole in her brain. Why, Lord, did she have to start this conversation tonight of all nights? She should have waited. Then she wouldn't have to battle everything inside of her at once. She'd waited all week for him to come home, want her, and not be tired. Now she'd messed up. No, correction: he'd messed up!

Kenny's footsteps followed her down the hall. How was she supposed to be in the mood now, when the man just dismissed her innermost dreams? She'd wanted to make love to him in the worst way . . . had removed all obstacles, had done her best to make the

...thing romantic, fixed his favorite food, got the kids squared away, took a shower, put on her favorite lotion and gown, gave him a bath, and *now* look at the evening.

She wrapped her arms around herself, trying to still the conflicting emotions as she heard him enter the bedroom behind her. Just once, Lord, it would be so nice if her husband would make an evening special for her. She closed her eyes and steadied her breath. What would it be like to go out to do something she truly loved, and then come home to someone who'd prepared a nice meal, set the table, maybe brought home some flowers . . . got the kids squared away so that she could sit down . . . drew a hot, sensuous bath for her . . . and made love to her slow and easy and then with gusto? And not just annually on their anniversary—if then? Didn't he know how precious life was, how unpredictable it could be?

She opened her eyes and sucked her teeth. *Yeah, get a hold of yourself, girl, you're tripping.* She kept her back to him and fixed her gaze on the bed, where she'd turned down the sheets and spritzed them with the perfume he liked. What was the point? He probably didn't notice that, either.

"Maxine, baby, come on," Kenny said in a quiet voice as he slipped into the bedroom behind her and shut the door, and then latched the slide lock behind them. "If you want to write, then fine. Let's not argue—not tonight."

But he wasn't hearing her. There was no need to lock the door tonight. She sat down on the bed and gave him her back to consider. *Yeah, let's not argue on the night that would be most inconvenient to you.* But her needs or dreams or worries could wait until it was convenient for everyone else in the family—right? She could feel resentment bubbling in her, threatening to boil over.

The bed depressed beside her, and she could feel Kenny's moist warmth near her. A touch singed her arm as his rough palm glided over it. Instead of igniting excitement, the touch elicited the urge to shrug him away. She made herself sit very, very still.

"See," he murmured, "we don't have to get into an argument about this, honey. If you need to get out for one night a week, that's cool."

His tone sounded patronizing. Or was she reading too much into it? She shifted her body so she could look at him.

"Kenny," she began, "I'll need your support while I try this." He took her hand in his, and she felt safe to press on. "I'll need some time to think at night, to do homework from the class, and to polish—"

"Maxine," he said in a weary tone that annoyed her, "look, I don't mind you going to a class, but, in truth, I really don't have it in me to go through a lot of household chaos right now." He dropped her hand, stood, and walked over to his dresser to search for a pair of pajamas. "I'm in the process of building the business, and this new contract with the city is paramount. My hours fluctuate based on tow volumes, I have more responsibility and men to account for, the paperwork is a bear, and when I come home, I'm beat. So if you want to take the class, Maxine, take the class—but please do not start something right now that is going to cause a bunch of logistical problems. It's just your timing, baby."

Timing? Who knew what time anyone had left on the planet? She watched him root through his bureau and yank on his pajamas—a sure sign that he was going to hit the sack and simply go to sleep. Fury rumbled in the pit of her stomach. Just because she insisted that she be allowed to also pursue something of interest to her, now they had to have a spat, and now he was going to just go to sleep and forget about it? Like hell.

"My timing?" She was back on her feet as he slipped into bed beneath the covers without a word and clicked off the light on his nightstand.

He didn't answer. Silence made her want to snatch the covers from him, but she restrained herself. Instead, she walked over to the bedroom door and coolly unlocked it. The action got his attention.

"Let me ask you this," she proffered. "When would be the *right* time to try anything on my own?"

He let his breath out in a heavy, annoyed rush—but he was looking at her, not ignoring her. "Not when Chadway Towing just received its first major government contract."

She sat down on her side of the bed and yanked the covers back. "Next year, then?"

"Maybe," he grumbled, turning away from her, his gaze going toward the unlocked bedroom door.

"Or perhaps in eighteen more years, once all the kids are grown?" Her voice was filled with sarcasm.

"Now you're exaggerating."

She watched his breathing slow. He had the nerve to be trying to fall asleep on her—just to block out

her words, her thoughts, her feelings, with uncon-
sciousness!

She got under the covers and sat up with her back
pressed against the headboard. "Exaggerating?"

"Maxine, please. I've got a long day tomorrow, and I
have to get up early in the morning."

Yeah, right. He would have stayed awake to make
love, but since that clearly wasn't going to happen, all of
a sudden he's *tired*. "Like I didn't? Like I don't?"

"I didn't say that."

"But that's what you were implying. You work; I
don't. What you do is more important than what I do,
right?"

"Baby, you know that's not what I said."

"But that's what you meant."

Her arms folded themselves over her chest, and her
breathing came in short bursts of sudden fury.

"I'm going to sleep."

"We need to talk."

"We can talk about it tomorrow."

"No. I want to discuss this *now*. Why do I always
have to wait for an audience with you? Why is it that
when there's something important on my mind, it has
to wait? When something has *you* upset, we have to
deal with it when *you* want to—so why doesn't the same
hold true for me?"

Kenny rolled over and sat up, leaning his head
against the wall behind them with his eyes closed. Why
did a man have to go around Robin's bend to get to the
bottom of a problem with a woman? If there was something on her mind, Maxine needed to just spit it out.
All this back-and-forth, cat and mouse, long winding

road to get to what could be said in one direct straight line—that's what he could never understand. Kenny summoned his patience.

"Listen, Maxine. I have to get up in the morning, and—"

"I get up before you do, every morning God sends," she spat back. "Your coffee is made before your feet hit the floor. My day runs from five-thirty A.M. until eleven-thirty at night." Tears were now streaming down her cheeks in a hot, angry torrent as she faced him, and he opened his eyes to glare at her. "I make sure that *every* person in here has what *they* need to begin and go through *their* day!"

When he opened his mouth to offer protest, she quickly cut him off.

"And, I, too, am in constant motion throughout the day. Nobody lays my clothes out. Nobody sees to it that my laundry is done, my lunch is packed, my dinner is hot and waiting for me, the house clean—or that the children are all in order with homework done, hair combed, permission slips signed. You think about that, Kenneth."

Oh, shit. His wife had used his formal name. This was serious. Maybe it was that time of the month, and he'd lost track. Maybe that's why she was so off the hook about doing what was routine. But what had set her off like this?

"Baby . . . listen—"

"Don't patronize me, Kenneth Chadway!"

He watched her fling herself out of the bed and begin walking in a circle. Perhaps he shouldn't have turned his back to her and turned out the light.

Hmmm. Okay. Patting the side of the bed gently, he tried a different approach.

"Come back to bed, baby, so we can talk. I was just tired and wasn't hearing you. I'm sorry."

She stared at him for a moment, and he was pretty sure that her face began to relax a bit as she unfolded her arms, looked at the spot his hand patted, and sighed. Maybe . . .

"I just want to be given the same courtesies as the other people in this household are given."

She had spoken, but she hadn't moved toward the bed.

"Maxine, you're a wonderful mother and wife." Dates began to form in his mind. Was it near their anniversary? Did he forget some special day? Was she just getting stir-crazy? Maybe he could take her out to dinner, or something. Yeah, that had to be it. They hadn't been out one-on-one in a while, and maybe Maxine was feeling underappreciated. "Come on, baby. You know we love you."

As soon as he'd said the words, new tears formed in her eyes and trailed down her face. Lord have mercy. It had to be some hormonal thing making his wife act like this.

"Baby, don't cry. Take the class. Come to bed. Let's get some rest. There's no need to argue about something you want to do."

Just as suddenly as the tears had flowed, they seemed to stop as she angrily wiped them away.

"You are not getting this, Kenny. I'm not having some kind of snit, or some momentary lapse of sanity." Her arms folded over her chest again, and her voice became strong and clear. "I want respect. I need to follow my dreams for once—and finish something I started, successfully."

"Respect?" It was all he could do not to scratch his head. What the hell was she talking about?

"Yes. Respect."

Silence stood between them like a bedroom referee.

"Kenny, you have no idea what it is like to always take care of people and not have them think about *your* needs."

Was his wife insane? Didn't he just tow about fifty cars today with his crew? Did he not just put in a fifteen-hour day, with another one on the horizon?

"That's not true, Maxine, and you know it. I put in long days, and pay the bills around here without fail. I take care of *everyone* in this household."

He hadn't meant his voice to rise, but he was tired, and his wife was truly pissing him off. Why did this have to happen tonight? Everything was going according to Hoyle, was smooth, and they could have made love and gone to sleep. Desire and fatigue were making it difficult to think, much less argue. Why did women always start something when things were smooth?

"That's just the thing," she said calmly—too calmly. "You think because you pay the bills, that that is all there is to it."

Now he knew she was crazy. He would not be baited into an argument tonight. He wanted to make love, not fight. Obviously, that wasn't going to happen, so he just wanted to go to sleep.

"That is what you think, right, Kenny?"

That did it. "Do you have any idea what I did today, Maxine?"

"Do you have any idea what *I* did today?"

His gaze narrowed on her. Something fragile within him snapped. He was wide awake now. "Not a clue," he replied with sarcasm. "Tell me, what was so hard about your day, Maxine? Were you under trucks on your back on asphalt in the cold? Huh?" Somehow his legs had found their way to the side of the bed and had propelled him out of it. "Did you come in here so beat up that you didn't know if you could stand up and put the key in the front door? I do that so you and the kids don't have to worry about a thing in here—you have no idea what goes on down at Chadway during the day."

"Not true," she replied evenly, and got into the bed to leave him standing in the middle of the floor by himself. "I used to work down there, remember?"

Now she wasn't fighting fair, and he knew that he'd crossed the argument line. The invisible demilitarized zone.

"Baby . . . I don't resent working for you and the family. That's not what I meant. And, yeah, you were a big help to me at Chadway when you pitched in." He moved toward the bed with caution and sat on his side of it, speaking to her back.

She turned out her nightstand light. Oh boy.

"You work for the family," she said in a defeated murmur, "but it's also something that you take great pride in and love to do: owning your own business that you can watch grow. I'm proud of you for what you've accomplished, and very appreciative to have a husband who works hard to support his family."

He wasn't sure how it had happened, but her praise

contained so much resignation in it that it made him feel guilty. He knew that somehow he'd hurt her. He needed to make it right, at least for now. He also needed rest. He slid under the sheets again and wrapped his arm around her waist, spooning her. Her body was rigid. "You want to take the class right away . . . okay." He kissed the nape of her neck, and still her body remained stiffened against his.

"I've always been there for you to gladly support whatever you wanted to do," Maxine said. Her voice was just above a whisper, and he had to strain to hear her.

"I know, baby. That's part of why I love you so much." He kissed her shoulder, but it didn't move. He heard her sniff.

"But whenever I want to do something, there's always a struggle."

How could he make her understand that playing at things, and dabbling at her little interests, wouldn't keep the lights on or pay the mortgage?

"There's no struggle here," he finally murmured, not knowing what else to tell her.

"Yes, there is. The sad part of it is, Kenny, you don't even know you're doing it."

Now, what was a man supposed to say to that? Weariness claimed him. God, women were so confusing.

"All I know is that I love you," he whispered against her hair, trying to assuage by touch whatever wound he'd inflicted. Her body relaxed and yielded, but not in passion. It was more like a defeated surrender.

"I love you, too," she replied with an exhausted sigh. "Good night."

Maxine listened to her husband let his breath out in frustration, and felt the bed move as he rolled away from her to pull the covers up over his shoulder. He just didn't get it.

When he'd started his business, she was there for him, rooting him on, rushing to fulfill every need, every convenience, to make his efforts soar. She had stood patiently in the background, making sure he had food, clothing, and a decent, clean, orderly home to return to—peace in his space so he could think, dream, and create. She'd scurried noisy children away from him, had been his sounding board for business problems, let him talk, and talk, and work out solutions with patience and diligence and love. She had concern for his goals and accomplishments. If Kenneth Chadway left the planet, he'd have something tangible for his kids to remember him by. Just like Bird would, and Lem one day might . . . and Teri most assuredly would. But she would just be Mom. She had taken care of all the details around Kenny's dream, and had not wavered.

All she wanted was half of that commitment back. A few nights to try to build something that made her heart soar. Was it too much to ask that she be given a little space to think, create, and do? Why couldn't she come home, for once, to a dinner made, children happily asleep with their homework done, lunches made, their clothes in order, and no dishes in the sink? One night, Lord. Why not? And why did she have to ask for *permission* to dream? Why did she have to ask for space to think? Why did it have to be a whole big deal just to have her husband stretch himself beyond his daily routine one night a week—after all the years she'd put in?

Why didn't he understand that she, too, was a person—not just the chief cook and bottle washer or maid?

Abruptly, Maxine sat up in bed, startling her husband enough to make him stare up at her.

"One night a week, Kenny, is all I'm asking for—and I shouldn't have even had to ask you. If you listened to me more often, or cared about the things that were important to me, this argument would not have been an argument. Period."

There. It had been said.

"I thought we'd discussed that you could take the class, and I'd said okay. So what's the problem now?"

She didn't like his tone—*at all.*

"The problem is this. For all these years, I have had your back. I want the same thing in return."

"Max—"

"No, don't cut me off. Hear me out."

"Maxine, it's late."

"Kenny, I'm not playing. Don't cut me off." She forged on. "We *both* work. True, your efforts yield a substantial check, mine don't. But that doesn't devalue what I do."

He sighed, and she wanted to slap him.

"When you were, and still are, pursuing your dreams, I take up the slack in that effort. That counts for something."

"Yes, it does, baby—"

"Don't speak to me with that 'yes baby' thing in your voice," she snapped.

He sighed again.

"You don't have to ask if your clothes are clean. They

are. You don't have to ask if your dinner is ready. It is. You don't ever have to worry about who cares for the children, or where they are or what they are doing. Like a genie in a lamp, things get done. You don't have to worry about the little things, as they are incorrectly termed, because they get done. Poof, like magic—so you can think and concentrate on your dream. That is what I am asking for in return—not just a few hours on a Wednesday night."

He sat up and stared at her. "You want me to go to my business, work like a Georgia mule all day, and then come home here and do all this other stuff, too? Just so you can dabble in this new idea of writing—something that pays nary a bill around here? Maxine, have you lost your mind?"

She stared at him, too stunned to even speak for a moment. Dabble? She felt so devalued, her voice came out as a whisper. "One night a week wouldn't kill you."

Kenny shook his head, sighed, and slid down under the covers again, his back toward her once more.

"I do it," she said evenly. "I have for years. Worked my normal day job here, plus pulled extra weight in the evenings."

"All right. Whatever you say, Maxine. I'm going to sleep."

She could feel her fingernails digging into her palms. "Because it was important to you, I took on extra responsibilities to assist you."

"Go to sleep, Maxine. This conversation is going nowhere."

Nowhere! What she had to say didn't matter, because

there was no money attached to her mission? Nowhere? She'd been dismissed? That was *it*.

"How many women work a day job, bring home a healthy salary, but still have to also do most, if not all, the household chores?"

"Thousands. Go to sleep."

"That's my point. But when the man is starting a new job, a new business, he gets to singularly focus on just that thing he wants to do. And, then, when it's successful, he *still* gets to have all the mundane things done for him—why? Because he's successful, and 'shouldn't have to'—right?"

"Maxine, I am tired and in no mood for rhetorical discussions. Take some Midol and lie down. I'm exhausted. I'm going to sleep. Good night."

"How can you sleep when we have to discuss this very fundamental issue?"

"Why do women always want to talk into the wee hours about some esoteric nonsense, when a man has to get up and go to work in the morning? I'm not playing, Maxine. Go to sleep—so I can."

"Esoteric nonsense? Did I hear you right, Kenneth?"

"Enough."

"Who do you think you're talking to? One of the children?"

"Maxine—"

"Oh, so you can just shut me up, blot out what I have to say, because you say so? I have no voice, no vote, no contribution to this household because I don't bring home the bacon?"

His silence might as well have been a slap across her face.

"Well, I'll tell you something, Mr. Chadway, I'm going to take my class. I'm going to have one night a week to pursue something important to me. And *you* figure out how to rustle up dinner that night. You see that *your* children have lunches for the next day. You find the baby-sitter. You make sure on that one Wednesday night a week that their homework gets done, that their needs are met and their clothes are readied for the next school day—yours, too, since you think I don't do shit around here all day but waste time. And then you can be there to give me a bath, and be all happy to see me when I come home—all showered, and ready to make love, after your day!"

She was stuttering, sputtering mad. "And, and, you wash the dishes, and put the food away so it doesn't spoil and give this family ptomaine poisoning, and you make sure there's something defrosted for that night—so this family can save money on take-out food, and so we can eat healthy. And *you* see how it feels, for once, to not have your sounding board there—to not have somebody give a rat's ass about what's on your mind—because I'll be too busy writing, doing my homework, to hear about it."

"Fine. Now can we go to sleep?"

"No, we can't go to sleep! I also want to inform you that since slavery has been abolished, and my little contribution over these years should be worth some remuneration, I'm buying myself a laptop computer tomorrow!"

"Maxine, we don't need to be wasting money because you're angry—"

"See? When I need or want something, it's a waste.

When anybody around here wants a fishing rod, a new bowling ball, a video game, it happens!" She was ready to leap from the bed with all the covers to find the sofa. "When was the last time I bought anything for *me?*"

"Buy a new dress, shoes, whatever, Maxine. At this point in the night, I really don't care."

She was out of the bed like lightning had struck her, snatching up her pillow and the comforter in one deft swoop.

"Where are you going?"

Kenny's lazy, nonchalant reply was like a dousing of ice water against her central nervous system.

"Nowhere!" she boomed, flinging the jumble of bed linen and the pillow at him. "*You* are going. Not me. I didn't start this!"

Kenny sat up slowly and gathered the ball of items in his arms with weary patience. His actions were so methodical that she thought she'd implode. He was treating her like she was deranged, and it shot a new level of adrenaline through her as he stood, stretched, yawned, and made his way to the door.

"Good night," he intoned flatly. "At least now I can get some real sleep."

She was so angry, she didn't know what to do with herself. For a full minute after the bedroom door quietly closed behind him, she paced back and forth like a trapped tiger. Of all the nerve. Of all the nerve! Who the hell did he think he was? No respect. Not a shred of understanding of what she was trying to say. Fury gave way to instantaneous fatigue, and bitter tears raced down her cheeks. Arrogance. Pure male arrogance. She fought back sobs, not even sure why she needed to cry so badly.

Tomorrow, she was buying her computer. Tomorrow, she was going to call her sisters. Tomorrow, she was going to find a baby-sitter. Tomorrow, life in the Chadway household was going to be different.

Change was not just in the damned wind; it lived here!

three

Kenny's back felt like someone had been beating him all night with a sledgehammer. He slowly sat up and swung his legs over the side of the sofa. Slightly disoriented, he rose and shuffled toward the kitchen, where a light appeared. As he walked he drew in a deep breath, half expecting to smell the aroma of coffee brewing. Slowly, it came back to him. He was in the doghouse—for an unexplained offense.

And there she was, sitting at the table, sipping tea, no coffee in the maker, scribbling on a legal pad. Maxine didn't even look up when he entered the room. This was not how he wanted things to be with his wife. What had kicked off this bizarre argument? She'd made all sorts of unfounded allegations—said he didn't respect her, which was totally untrue. Now the silent treatment. Why? Didn't she know life was too short to waste time not speaking to loved ones? Didn't she understand that anything could happen to either of them during the day, and some foolish argument might be the last thing they'd ever said to each other? Maxine wasn't making sense!

"Good morning," he grumbled. "Common courtesy to speak, isn't it?"

"Good morning," she said in a falsely chipper voice without stopping her task.

He stood in the middle of the floor and glanced up at the clock. Five-thirty A.M. What the hell was going on in his house? It was too early for this.

"Maxine, you getting the kids up for school?" He stared at her through bleary eyes, waiting on her to answer. He *knew* his wife wasn't going to make the children late for school just because they had an argument. And wasn't she going to make the coffee, or say anything about last night?

"They don't have to get up until six," she said calmly, her gaze never leaving the paper she was writing on. "This is *my time* in the morning—before the household wakes up."

She was ignoring him, offering up the semi-silent treatment. Okay, if that's how she wanted it. Besides, the urge to take a leak, and the need for a decent cup of coffee, competed with his desire to get a reasonable response from her. And the last thing he wanted was for one of the children to come downstairs and see that he'd been forced to be a refugee in his own home. Dad, a sofa sleeper? Not hardly. That was no way for a man to be treated in his own home.

"A man can't even get a cup of coffee in the morning without static," he grumbled, leaving the recalcitrant Maxine where she sat.

By the time Kenny came back downstairs to leave for work, the household was buzzing with activity, and

Maxine was the picture of efficiency. She was also not speaking beyond the necessary. "Yes, no, uh-huh, have a nice day," was all she was giving up. Didn't even kiss him good-bye. It made no sense. The kids were looking at him funny when he left the house. This was no way for a man to leave his house in the morning. Tonight they were gonna deal with this.

The garage had never felt so lonely as he pulled up to the empty lot in the frigid March air. Yet at the same time it looked like a port in a storm. At Chadway Towing, he was boss, was in control, and knew the lay of the land. No one had better start anything or get on his nerves today.

With indignation, he snatched up the bag of lunch Maxine had made. Opening it, he shook his head. A salad and a box of apple juice? Oh, see now, Maxine was really fighting dirty. Okay. Okay—fine! Kenny left the bag in the truck, and his heavy work boots hit the driveway gravel. He wasn't eating no damned salad for lunch.

The thud of his footfalls became heavier as his temper rose. All this drama, and for what? What in the world did he do? His hands found the huge ring of keys in his pocket, and he opened up for the day. Lack of caffeine was working his nerves, too. He turned on the lights and headed for his office, where his old coffeemaker could be found. The sound of a car in the driveway just annoyed him further. His brother-in-law was always on time, but this morning he needed a moment to himself.

Kenny hadn't even filled the pot with water before he heard Lem's boots stomp across the floor, followed by his daily salutation.

"Yo, Kenny!"

"Yeah, yeah, yeah. Coffee'll be ready in a minute."

He didn't even turn around to look at Lem. He didn't feel like talking about anything this morning. What was there to say, really?

"And good morning to you, too," Lem said, upbeat and cheerful.

Kenny glanced up briefly and began loading in the filter and heaping grounds into the small unit. Lem was leaning against the door frame with a wide smile. Right. It was Thursday morning, and his brother-in-law was a married man, too. Lem's wide grin pissed him off. Why couldn't things just be normal in his own home? Was that too much for a man to ask for?

"Tow sheets from the city are over on the front desk. No new call-ins yet—but if you want to get started on the city list, that would work."

"Can't a man get a hello and a cup of coffee first?" Lem chuckled, shook his head, and pushed himself off the door frame to find a clean mug. "What's up, Kenny? It's too nice a day to start off all out of sorts."

Kenny watched the coffee brew. "Be ready in a minute," he repeated, not wanting to discuss anything beyond the mundane.

"No doubt," Lem said, handing Kenny a mug. "You cool, man? Everything all right?"

"Why are you in my face, first thing in the morning? Huh? Can't a man just have a cup of coffee in the morning?"

Lem sighed, poured himself a cup of the dark brew, rooted around for the sugar, and shrugged. "No problem, man. Just checking on your vibe."

"My *vibe* is *fine*."

Kenny poured himself a mug and sat down heavily in his desk chair, focusing his gaze on the swirling dark liquid in his cup. He took a deep sip from it, closed his eyes, and made a face. To his dismay, Lem sat down across from him, peering over the rim of his own mug at him.

"What, Lem?"

"Nothing. You just seem out of sorts."

"I'm not out of sorts. I'm just tired."

"Okay. My bad." Lem took a slow sip and made a face, too, and then set his mug down on the edge of Kenny's desk. "Brother-in-law, I'm gonna buy you a new coffeemaker."

"Well, since Maxine is off buying laptop computers, I guess I could use the donation to the business—since what I do around here isn't good enough for anybody."

Lem looked at him for a long time as Kenny shuffled papers from pile to pile on his desk. He didn't have time for this crap this morning.

"I know she didn't say that, Kenny—that's not Maxine's way." Lem stood and collected his cup of coffee like a person fleeing the scene of an accident.

"Oh, no? Then what do you call it?" Kenny was almost on his feet.

"My name is Bennett, and I ain't in it. Besides, I don't even know what you're talking about—so I'm gonna mind my business."

"Best thing in the world for a man to do," Kenny shot back. "But I know what she said. I'm not deaf."

Lem hovered by the door and pondered the situation. This was Kenny's way. He never asked for advice directly, and Lord knows, not a soul on earth could give it to him. But when his brother-in-law began the conversation in the middle, he was expecting his family, especially his boy, to have his back. Lem sighed. This was a delicate situation, and he had to approach it with respect.

Taking another sip from his mug, Lem leaned on the door frame again. "Aw, man, go 'head. What did she say that was so bad? Huh?"

There. It was out on the floor. It was Kenny's opening to tell his side of it while saving face.

"What did she say? What did she *say!*"

Lem waited.

"She's talking crazy, man. She's taking some Wednesday-night class for writing."

The two men looked at each other. Kenny was now standing, leaning on his knuckles on his desk. Lem rubbed his jaw.

"Whew," Lem offered, letting his breath out slow but hard. "Wednesday nights are tough, brother."

"You're telling me," Kenny fussed, pushing away from his desk to walk back to get more coffee.

"Kicked up a lot of dust in my house when I started taking that twelve-week class for entrepreneurship."

"Yeah. Created a lot of strain on the environment, as I recall."

"Truth. But after a while Bird got used to it and started supporting me."

Kenny's gaze narrowed on Lem. "Oh, so now I don't support my wife?"

Lem held his hands out in front of him. "Aw, Kenny, man, you know better than that. You support your family better than most men I know. I am the last person who would go there with you."

This one was major, and talking to Kenny this morning was like shaking a red cape in front of a bull.

"Thank you," Kenny finally said in a begrudging tone as he sat heavily.

Lem knew that the immediate storm had passed, and maybe Kenny would talk. His brother-in-law seemed to chill somewhat, now that he'd complimented his ability to support his household. But with Kenny like this, one never knew when he'd blow again.

"She's not just taking this class, man," Kenny said in a disgusted tone. "She's talking about homework, and *assignments* that will eat into the week, and me having to come home from a hard day at what we do here and do all that house stuff—for six weeks, mind you. Dinner, dishes, kids, lunches, and whatnot."

Lem chuckled. "Was that before or after you pissed her off?"

Kenny looked at him hard, then looked away, and suddenly chuckled. "You know Maxine well."

"Brother-in-law, what did you say to her that made her snap?"

"Nothing. That's just it. Nothing." Kenny stood and started pacing in a tight line behind his desk, using his hands to punctuate his statements. "And all of a sudden she's talking about hypothetical other women's jobs, the load they carry and so forth, and I wind up on the sofa with *a salad* for lunch."

"Nooooo," Lem said, stifling a chuckle. "A salad, man? From Maxine's kitchen—for you?"

"This is what I'm saying." Kenny stood there with

his arms open and his eyes wide. "You hear me?"

This time Lem did shake his head. "You gotta make this right, Kenny. A salad and the sofa—in March? Seriously. You gotta dig deep and figure this one out."

Both men stared at each other as a silent understanding passed between them.

"I don't know what's wrong with her," Kenny finally said.

"All right. Take it from the top. She wanted to take a class—some time away from the family for herself, right?"

Kenny nodded, as though talking to a doctor who was going through a complex diagnosis. "That part I got."

"Okay," Lem pressed on, entering the office just a bit more. "Then some words got exchanged, and she felt like you didn't hear her. Right?"

"Something like that," Kenny admitted as Lem sipped his coffee. "She got all worked up about not being appreciated."

Lem put a finger to his lips and studied the floor. "Brother-in-law, when's the last time you took Maxine out to dinner—with just the two of you?"

Their eyes met.

"Been a while, hasn't it?"

For a moment, Kenny didn't answer.

"When's the last time she just went out shopping with her girls?"

Again, Kenny didn't answer, but he summoned a defense up from his gut. "Maxine always says she doesn't need anything—she's practical, like me, and doesn't go in for all that. Besides, she never goes anywhere to wear any fancy stuff."

Lem set down his coffee mug on a metal file cabinet and folded his arms over his chest. "You hear what you just said to me?"

Kenny hesitated. "Aw, man, Lem. I messed up, didn't I?"

"You bring her a five-dollar bunch of flowers from the deli lately—just because?"

Kenny shook his head.

"You say, 'Baby, why don't you let me catch these dishes tonight,' once in a while?"

Kenny took a breath to argue, but Lem jumped in.

"Not because you don't work hard, but just to give her her props for working hard, too?"

Kenny cast his gaze toward the filing cabinets.

"All I'm saying, man, is this: an ounce of prevention is worth a pound of cure. I learned the hard way. Now, instead of a fifty dollar pair of shoes, you're in for a laptop."

Kenny chuckled sadly and shook his head. "You ain't lying, brother."

"Now, instead of twenty minutes to wash the dishes for her every now and again, she's taking a class. I told you you should read her poems and stuff with more regularity. I hate to say it."

Kenny's shoulders sagged with defeat. "Maybe I'll take her out to dinner this weekend, or somethin'."

"I'm out," Lem said in a cheerful voice, backing through the door. "Last thing I'm gonna say is, the weekend is three days away. If you know like I know, you won't wait that long."

"Teri, I didn't call for that," Maxine insisted, trying to get her older sister to understand. "I know you have one, and I just wanted to find out what kind of laptop to buy—I didn't call to ask you to buy one for me."

"Well, Maxine, I think you deserve the best for what you're trying to do—and it is high time that you do something for *yourself* over there. You have a right to buy something to further your career goals. Kenny is a good provider, and Lord knows I love him—and he's a much better husband than what Bird has to deal with—but still, you should get the best. Why are you always skimping on things for yourself, honey?"

Maxine sighed and sat in a kitchen chair. She was not about to go into the whole argument she and Kenny had just been through, because her older sister would probably want to send out a posse. Maybe even set up a full-scale intervention, knowing Teri. All she needed was some technology assistance.

"Teri," Maxine said as patiently as she could, "I don't need to break the bank. All I need is something that I can write on."

She heard her sister release a breath of frustration through the receiver.

"You have a right to indulge yourself."

Maxine laughed. "I am. Trust me. Just to have my own computer is an indulgence. But I don't need to buy something that costs thousands of dollars; I just need something functional."

"If the money is the prob—"

"I love you, too. But no, Teri. This is a matter of principle."

Silence crackled on the telephone between them for a moment. Maxine could feel her breathing escalating, and words tumbled from her mouth that she'd sworn to herself she wouldn't allow to fall out. But just thinking about her argument with Kenny was making her angry all over again.

"I am an equal contributor to this household, and Kenny needs to truly respect that. It's a matter of respect. And while I am pissed off beyond comprehension, I'm not buying something just for the sake of buying it. If you don't know what make and model I should buy, that's fine. And thank you for helping me with what you did know."

"Okay," Teri said carefully, cautiously, as if she were talking a crazy person down from a high-rise building ledge. "I can recommend a model a few steps down that will meet your needs—but Max, why are we discussing laptops when we should be addressing what's really bothering you?"

"Bothering me? Bothering me? Nothing's bothering me, Teri. I'm just fine. I just need some assistance with my purchase before I make it—I don't want to get ripped off by some techno-weenie at the store. But I'm fine."

"You sound stressed, Max," Teri murmured. "Have you spoken to Bird yet?"

"I am not stressed!" Maxine shouted. "Why do I have to be stressed just because I want to take a class, for God's sake? Huh? These people around here can just—"

"Maxine. Listen to yourself, honey. You are wigging out."

"I am so damned mad, Teri, I could spit nails, is what I am."

"Okay. What happened?"

"Nothing happened, Teri—nothing at all. That's the problem. It's the same ole, same ole, and I want to write, but it's some big joke to everybody . . . let little Maxine *dabble* in her *hobby.*"

Teri's gasp passed through Maxine's skeleton.

"Noooo . . . ," Teri whispered. "My brother-in-law did not go there. Oh, Lord have mercy, Maxine."

"I know . . ." Suddenly Maxine's throat felt tight and filled with tears, making it hard for her to speak.

"I'm putting Bird on this call—three-way."

"No. Don't get Bird in the middle of this, Teri. She'll be all high-strung about it."

"I am calling Bird right this minute. You need backup. A united front."

Maxine closed her eyes as she heard Teri click off and then immediately come back on the line.

"Max," Bird hollered, "what did Kenny say!"

Maxine groaned.

"He said," Teri repeated, "that Max was dabbling in some hobby, and he's being unsupportive about her taking the class."

"Girl," Bird fussed, "you need to show him rather than tell him."

"That's right, Bird," Teri piped in. "Our sister doesn't have to stand for that."

"That's right. Since his big rusty behind doesn't appreciate you, then let him fix his own food and wash his own clothes. Go on strike."

Now Maxine laughed. "Go on strike? Bird—see, Teri, this is why I said not to call—"

"Oh, no. It's on now," Bird railed.

"How am I supposed to go on strike with *babies* in the house? Pullease," Maxine scoffed.

"Shoot," Bird continued, undaunted. "I would fix my *children's* lunch, wash *their* clothes, and take *them* to McDonalds or for pizza when *they* came home from school, and when he came home, there wouldn't be *jack* in the oven or defrosted. You hear me?"

"Mama used to say, you can show 'em better than you can tell 'em," Teri offered. "And what did Daddy say? 'You never miss your water till your well runs dry.' "

"Would be bone, desert dry around my house—trust me. In the bedroom, too," Bird added as she chuckled, making them all laugh.

"I never used that as weapon against Kenny," Maxine said, growing concerned. "I mean, that's not really fair . . . and, I don't know about all that other stuff. I just want to buy my laptop, go to class, and have things be smooth."

Then her crazy sisters began chanting, "Strike, strike, strike," until Maxine howled with laughter.

"No justice, no peace," Bird laughed through the receiver. "Don't be a scab and cross your own picket line, girl."

"But—"

"Listen," Bird said with impatience. "I keep my salon open until nine on Wednesday nights—so you just bring my nieces and my nephew by my shop right after school. The baby will be passed around to all the girls, you know that. Kelly and Ahmad can get their homework done in my office and watch TV, and also help out with little odd jobs and stuff, and I can swing by your house on the way home to drop them off. By that time Kenny will be there, and we always order in food for all the Cut It Up staff, so the children will be fed. Mr. Chadway can fend for himself, since he's so stubborn. Right, Teri?"

"That's right. And some of those nights, I could swing by and get the kids from Bird's shop, feed them, and make sure they are home and in bed early, if that's a concern. A few weeks won't kill me to help my sister do something that is important to her—unlike Mr. Chadway."

"These men don't know," Bird huffed. "The Joseph sisters can close ranks like *that.*" Her fingers delivered a crisp snap through the receiver.

Her sisters' support made Maxine swallow hard. They believed so much in her, and were so ready to turn their lives upside down just to pitch in. She didn't know what to say other than, "I love you guys." They were more than sisters, they were her friends . . . and that was all she'd wanted from her husband. It became so crystal clear in that moment. She wanted her husband to be her friend again. She now had words to articulate her feelings. As usual, the roundabout way to getting to the root of things had happened, in the female process of problem solving.

"We love you, too," her sisters chimed in before Maxine could speak.

"Strike!" Bird hollered with a laugh.

"Well, Max, it's your decision," Teri said, "but you've got Kenny spoiled rotten."

"He is sorta used to having things his way, but he's a good—"

"Kenny is spoiled rotten, and you know it, Max," Bird went on. "Just rotten, and you don't put your foot down—*ever.* How long is this class?"

"Six weeks."

"And he's fussing because you want to go out for six evenings? He needs to stop," Teri urged. "Oh, he just needs to stop."

"It doesn't bring in any income. In fact, I'm about to spend a sizable amount on a computer," Maxine said in a quiet voice. "Maybe I shouldn't."

"Make her stop, Bird, before I scream," Teri implored. "Any income? What has *that* got to do with it? With all that you do around there? If you ever become a novelist, you could make six figures or better! Consider it an investment—like a student loan, if you must—but get the damned computer."

"Now I know y'all are tripping." Maxine laughed self-consciously.

"She's not," Bird added. "You've never even given yourself a chance to try anything you really wanted to do without a bunch of resistance from the peanut gallery over there. Be honest."

The line went silent. All that could be heard was background noise from Teri's office and Bird's salon.

"I just wanted him to understand like you guys do— just wanted him to be my friend, and be supportive like you all are being right now—but I couldn't get him to hear me. That's why I was so upset." Maxine drew her breath in slowly and let it out in a rush. "He always wants me to just give him the short version of what I'm trying to say, but sometimes it takes time to form the thought, to express what I mean in full."

"Right," Bird said in a huff, "you wanted a discussion, not some quickie statement of 'just the facts, ma'am.' " Men never get that part—that a conversation is a process, and feelings are involved." Bird sucked her teeth. "They think you're wasting time, when what you're doing is working out the issue while you're talking and thinking out loud—and then they cut you off."

"Exactly," Maxine said, closing her eyes as validation swept through her.

"Did he even ask you why you want to do this, what was really in your heart?"

Maxine could hear Bird and Teri breathing as they allowed her the time to respond. "No," Maxine whispered. "He was jumping either right to a solution or to who was at fault, but he never asked me why writing was so important now. I couldn't think or get it out, with him firing one-liner questions at me."

"Uhmmm-hmmm . . . ," Bird said, her voice blending with Teri's.

"I just want something to leave behind more permanent than me," Maxine said. "There's been so much tragedy, and so many near misses. . . . I keep thinking of Mom, and what I'd give to be able to read anything she had to say—something that would let me hear her voice again, and . . . Oh, I don't know."

Silence fell between the sisters as each became absorbed in their own thoughts.

"I understand," Bird said, quietly assuring her.

"Case closed," Teri announced after a moment. "I'll give you the makes and models that will do the trick. Bird and I will help spot you for baby-sitting those nights, and you deal with your spoiled husband's attitude. No justice, no peace."

Through the kitchen window, Maxine watched the

effects of the strong March winds. Change was blowing hard, and coming in like a lion.

When Kenny walked in the house, only the kitchen light was on. It was quiet—too quiet. Scary quiet.

He stood at the front door inside the foyer and glanced around. At eight P.M., his house was never this silent. He smelled the air. No trace of dinner.

"Hey, everybody!"

Not a sound echoed back except his own voice. Aw, man, what was up now?

Then he heard paper rustle in the kitchen, and he tensed. He looked around to see if there had been any signs of a break-in, and picked up the steel baseball bat he kept stashed by the front door. Then he walked quietly toward the kitchen.

He immediately saw Maxine sitting alone at the table, loading software on a shiny new, flat black computer. He relaxed his home-protection stance, but his tension was replaced by pure indignation.

"Hello!"

"Good evening, Kenneth."

She hadn't even looked up.

"Didn't you hear me hollering to you from the other room?"

"Yes."

"And?"

"I was busy trying to figure this out."

He counted to ten in his mind.

"Where are the kids?"

"Over at Teri's."

"Did they eat?"

"Yes. At McDonalds. Aunt Teri treated."

Kenny stared at his wife. Oh, so it was like that, now? The Joseph sisters had obviously closed ranks again. Now he was really mad.

"Well, isn't it kinda late for the kids to be out, especially the baby?"

"Ahmad usually doesn't go to bed until ten or eleven; Kelly has a field day tomorrow and doesn't have homework. The baby will fall asleep in Teri's car when she brings them all home, and she can nap during the day while I'm writing. They are due home at nine."

Maxine's blasé tone grated on him. She was blowing him off and acting sedate and calm, when this was no calm situation. He was tired and hungry and had worked all day under the stress she'd started last night. Women.

"So you didn't make dinner, I take it?" He could feel his blood pressure going up to create a ringing in his ears.

"Nope. Had other things to do."

Other things to do! What, was she on strike or something crazy? He stared at his wife hard. "Have you eaten?"

"Yup. Since nobody else ever cares to see that my needs are met, I've gotten used to fending for myself." Maxine slipped a diskette into the laptop, still not looking at Kenny. "I had a salad."

"You know, Maxine, this has gone far enough."

She held up her hand without even glancing at him, her vision glued to the computer screen. "Yes. It has. But to clear up any possible misconceptions about what I'm doing, I have met all *my* commitments to people who cannot fend for themselves. *Their* clothes are clean. *Their* homework is done. *They* have eaten. *Their* home environment is clean. Now I am working on something that requires *my* attention. You are intruding on *my* personal space."

His wife had lost her mind. Kenny shifted from foot to foot, nervous but angry. She had a helluva nerve. What if he just paid for the people in his household who couldn't fend for themselves—like only for the kids' clothes, only for their food, only enough utilities for *their* needs, and he left Maxine naked and starving in the streets? This was no way to run a home.

"And what about us? We need to talk," he finally grumbled.

"Later, when it is convenient for me. Isn't that how it works for you? Last night you went to sleep and didn't want to talk. Right now, I don't want to talk."

"Maxine, I'm not playing."

For the first time since he walked into the room, she looked up at him. He dropped the bat off onto the floor and folded his arms over his chest. Now they were getting somewhere.

"Do I look like I am *playing*, Kenneth?"

Her gaze was so lethal that he was tempted to glance away. Oh, shit . . . this was really bad. No, Maxine was not playing.

"Uh, Maxine, baby, listen . . . I don't want to keep this thing going like this. Now you've made your point, and you've spent a bunch of money, but the kids are out in the streets—"

"First of all," she said from a low place in her throat, "the children are with my sister, and are not 'out in the streets,' as you say." Her words seethed past her lips in a slow, punctuated stream. "Second of all, I'm not 'making a point.' I need this laptop for what I'm about to embark upon, and I've done what a responsible parent is supposed to do: namely, made sure my children are in reliable care while I work. Third, since I never spend money on anything, and this is a tool of my craft, I haven't just 'spent a bunch of money' on nonsense. Lastly, about money, I will say this: I should be able to occasionally spend personal money, based upon the fact that I am a contributing member of this household."

When he opened his mouth to speak, she cut him off. "But since what I do has no value to you, because there is no paycheck attached to it, then I can only assume that you don't need my services. Suit yourself. I have better things to do with my valuable time than waste it where it isn't valued. Now, if you will excuse me, I have a new system to boot up and get operable before my children come home. Good night."

Maxine lowered her laser beam gaze back to her computer and shunned him.

Dumbfounded, Kenny stood stock still for a moment, trying to gather his thoughts. Anger tore at him, but he also remembered Lem's chide.

"So, how long am I supposed to sleep on the sofa, huh? I'm supposed to just take up residence in the living room, is that it?"

"Nope."

"No what, Maxine?"

"You can sleep wherever you like. Upstairs, downstairs. I really don't care."

Her nonchalance was driving a crowbar through his temple. What did she mean, she didn't care where he slept? He could feel an interminable dry spell in the offing. Aw, maaaan . . .

"I came in here to see if you wanted to go out to dinner on Friday or Saturday night, but since you aren't speaking . . ."

He waited. It was a white flag. *C'mon, Maxine* . . .

"Thank you for the considerate offer," she said in an even tone, still fiddling with her new computer. "But I'll pass."

"Why!"

"I'm not interested in having dinner with a man who thinks what I'm doing is a foolish hobby. And I really have nothing to talk about—if someone doesn't hear what I have to say, anyway. Makes the conversation a little one-sided at dinner, you know? So why would I want to go anywhere, or do anything, with some man who treats me like that?"

"I'm not *some man*. I'm your *husband!*"

"That's an even worse indictment—the fact that my husband acts as if what I have to say is not worth listening to. I thought I had a friend as well as a husband, but I guess I was wrong. Whatever."

"Whatever? Maxine. Would you stop playing with that machine and look at me so we can talk?"

"No."

"No?"

"No. I told you I had things to do; this conversation is not a priority for me right now. I have things to do that are more important than resolving this issue, hearing your angst, your drama, or caring about how you feel on the matter. Friendships have to be two-sided to work. This one doesn't. You'll get used to it. I did."

"This conversation is going nowhere, I can see."

"Precisely," she said in a forced chipper tone, thoroughly grating him.

"Well, what's here to eat, since you're not speaking or cooking?"

"Lunch meat. Salad. Bread, I think. Everything else is frozen."

"Oh, so now I have to go out of my own house and spend good money in the streets to eat?"

"No," she said with a patronizing sigh. "Like I told you. There's some lunch meat, bread—"

"Forget it!"

Vindicated. Hollow win though it was, Maxine tried not to chuckle as she listened to Kenny stomp through the house and slam the front door behind him.

Her dreams *would* be respected in this house. "Strike."

four

the next evening, Maxine looked at the kitchen wall clock and pulled out her pan of baked chicken. She couldn't run her household on perpetual strike; it wasn't good for the children. One night had been hard enough. She wasn't going to splinter the family routine of eating dinner together and sharing their days across the table with food.

Teri didn't understand, because she didn't have any kids yet. Bird could still play those games, because her son, little Jay, was still at the age of oblivion. However, Kelly and Ahmad would feel the icy vibes. They would wonder why the family routine had changed, want to know why Daddy didn't eat with them, why Daddy was doing his own laundry, want to know why their parents walked by each other with evil looks on their faces. And she was definitely not going to allow her children to live in a pigsty, no matter how angry Kenneth Chadway made her. Some things weren't done.

She began making the gravy for the mashed potatoes as she peered into the pot of string beans. She wasn't feeding her children fast food all the time, even if Bird and Teri were buying it. Consistency—that was the key. Her mama had been consistent, even when her daddy had his moments of lapse. Her mother didn't make the whole family suffer, just because she might have been annoyed at her spouse. Neither would she. And the last thing she wanted to have on her conscience was sending Kenny to an early grave by allowing him to eat any old thing out in the street.

Maxine wiped her flour-coated hand on the dish towel over her shoulder. Friday nights were normally filled with laughter, rented movies from Blockbuster, good food—just like Sundays. Tonight Ahmad had a dance, and the rest of them could sit up and have fun until the littlest ones fell asleep . . . waiting on their teenage son to come back through the door. She was not sending her son out of the house worrying about his parents.

"Grace," Maxine told herself. "Handle your responsibilities with grace." Don't make the children suffer, do not rob them of their wonder years or steal the joy from the family because of something that will pass. *Do not rob your children.* They had a good father. Kenny, with all his faults, was a good man. This was temporary "man shit." *Ignore his foolishness—but run your house, Maxine.*

When she heard Kenny come through the front door, she also heard him hesitate. *Yeah, I cooked, dammit.* He'd better recognize *all* that she did. *Your clothes are washed, too. You had a sandwich for lunch, even though you were too ornery to take it with you. Your house is clean, and your children are all home.* Her thoughts seized upon her anger, and she pushed it back, deep down into her consciousness. Not tonight. "Grace," she repeated in a whisper.

He couldn't believe it. He smelled dinner ready. Kenny glanced through the house as he hugged his daughters and tickled them. The table was set. Ahmad's boom box was blaring from upstairs. Peace had been restored. Maxine had come back to her right mind. His shoulders relaxed. Yeah, dammit; she'd better recognize his authority. That was no way to be running a house. Woman had to collect herself, get herself together.

Kenny paced toward the kitchen, leaving Kelly and the baby to play on the living room floor. He stood at the doorway for a moment, testing the waters before he opened his mouth. Maxine was busy at the stove and had glanced up with a pleasant expression on her face.

"How was your day?" she asked, like nothing had transpired between them during the last forty-eight hours.

Women.

"Fine," he muttered. "And yours?"

"Same ole, same ole," she said.

He noted there was no apparent sarcasm in her voice. But he also noted that her eyes looked sad, resigned. Somewhat defeated. He didn't like that look in her eyes; he missed the sparkle. He let his breath out slowly. Despite anything going temporarily awry, he loved this woman more than life itself. That's what he had to get Maxine to understand. When she'd said their friendship was one-way, he didn't like it at all. She'd always been his best friend—what had happened to change that?

He walked past her toward the refrigerator to get a beer but didn't stop to kiss her. The situation was still tenuous, at best. He noted the large lunch bag in there that he'd dismissed this morning. Another salad, probably. He'd been too angry before he'd left for work to even look in it. He took his beer out and closed the refrigerator door with a quiet thump.

"It was a pork chop sandwich, some fruit, a couple of brownies that I'd saved you from the tray I made for Kelly's field day, and a thermos of lemonade," she murmured, still working at the stove, reading his mind.

Damn . . . What could he say? His wife had saved brownies for him. She'd called a cease-fire, and he was still fighting.

"Thanks, baby," he said in a low, easy tone filled with regret. "Can we stop fighting tonight?"

"I already have, Kenny."

Her tone was gentle, not accusatory, but it felt like an indictment, nonetheless.

"I love you, baby. You know I appreciate you, right?"

She didn't answer verbally, just nodded. He would accept that for now.

"Why don't you wash up so we can all have dinner together?"

He nodded, took a swig from his beer, and brushed her cheek with a peck when he passed her again to go wash up.

It was one of the quietest dinners he'd shared with Maxine. Oh, the table was a flutter of noise and confusion, as usual, while each child clamored for his or her share of attention and food. But his wife sat there like a quiet,

serene ghost. Sure, she smiled, and interjected occasionally—but she wasn't *Maxine*. Her laughter was a light,
airy chuckle that stopped too soon. It didn't come from
down deep in her soul. Her eyes didn't crinkle at the
corners when she laughed with the children. In fact,
they never made contact with his during the entire
meal. He missed her so much.

There was no bob to her head, no sassy, quick-witted
comebacks aimed at their son. No teasing pinches given
to Kelly, just a gentle pat of her head. And the way she
cradled the baby in her lap, pulling their daughter from
the high chair to eat from her own plate. He'd watched
Maxine stroke the baby as though their little girl had
gotten a boo-boo within her heart.

He was sure that he saw tears glisten in Maxine's eyes
a time or two, and then burn away. But she was smiling
the whole time. A peaceful, Madonna-type smile. A
resigned-to-her-fate smile. The smile of a matriarch—
not the youthful, passionate, joyous, Maxine smile. He
had to fix this.

Ahmad was the first one to get up and move away
from the table, saying he had a dance. Kenny tried to
protest, but Maxine calmly reminded him that the boy
had been given permission to go a week ago. He
watched his wife stand and begin clearing the table with
the children. She walked so slowly to the kitchen and
back, it was almost like a death march, it seemed.

"Baby, let me help with the dishes," he offered.

She just shook her head. "I got it. You had a long
day and a long week."

The serenity of her placid response felt like hand-
cuffs. He stood, took his plate to the kitchen, and

began running dishwater in the sink, despite her protest.

"I still need the sink, honey," she murmured, nudging him out of the way. "I have to get the garbage off the plates first and then clean out the sink before I can run the water for the pots and pans. The plates and stuff can go in the dishwasher."

"Oh."

He stood there just staring at her for a moment, like a fish out of water. "Well, let me put the food up, then." He began rooting around in the cabinets, trying to find a Tupperware container, and drew a big one down.

"That won't fit in the refrigerator with all the other stuff," she said calmly, taking the plastic bowl from his hands, putting it back, and retrieving a smaller, more efficient-sized one in its stead.

"How about if I go get some movies?" he offered, knowing he was in her way.

"That'll be nice," she said without charge or emotion. "The little ones will enjoy that."

He remained in the doorway, hovering for a moment. "But what would *you* like to see?" He was trying his best, and what was at stake was too important. In his heart he really wanted to be more open to doing things her way for a change, but she wouldn't even look at him now.

Maxine shrugged. "Doesn't matter. Get whatever you think the children will like, or whatever you want to see."

Oh, boy . . . this was really bad. Maxine *loved* to watch movies.

"Baby, it doesn't matter to me. There are a lot of

things out now that we didn't catch in the theaters. I mean, I can pick up something that'll entertain Kelly, and the baby just likes the action. But after they go to sleep . . ."

"After they go to sleep," Maxine said on a tired exhale, "you can watch whatever you'd like, Kenny."

He tensed, trying to read into her comment. "You don't want to watch movies with me?"

"I didn't say that," she replied, her back to him as she busied herself around the kitchen. "I'll watch whatever you want to watch."

Oh, boy . . .

"We could just sit and talk and listen to some jazz, if you want. We don't have to watch movies." How did a man reverse himself out of a rut—especially when his wife didn't even seem to care any longer that he was attempting to make a change? It was a Catch-22. Kenny rubbed his palm over his scalp and waited for a sign, a way in.

Again, she shrugged and kept her gaze on the food she was storing away. "If that's what you'd like to do, I'll be happy to sit with you and hear about your day, Kenny. No problem."

At a loss, he shoved his hands in his pockets. "Want me to pick up some wine . . . for later, maybe?"

"If you'd like wine later, that's fine."

"Maxine, baby . . . I didn't say *I* wanted wine. I'm asking what you want. Do *you* want some wine for later?"

She shrugged her one-shoulder shrug. "Doesn't matter what I want. Whatever you want is fine, Kenny."

"Okay," he said in a quiet voice. "I'll pick up a good

movie for Kelly, and later, let's you and me talk over a glass of wine while Ahmad is out at his dance. What I really want," he said softly, "is peace."

She just nodded.

He watched her all during the movie, and to the untrained eye, there was nothing wrong. Maxine laughed with Kelly, squealed with the baby, and said "Eeiiiilll" at all the yucky parts of *Osmosis Jones*. She got his children off to bed with loving efficiency, read bedtime stories to their sleepy girls, and said prayers with them and over them, and he'd watched it all from their bedroom doors. He had a good wife. A loving, kind, generous wife. An angel in the flesh. What had he been thinking, to hurt Maxine's feelings?

The problem was, he didn't exactly know what had kicked it off, and he definitely didn't know how to make it right. But he would try to repair the rift between them the only way he knew how—wine, music, a little cuddle time on the couch. He loved her. Didn't Maxine know that? Maybe Lem had a point. It had been a long time since they'd spent some one-on-one time together—without children, without time pressures, without anything or anyone but them. Maybe they should go out on a date or something? But before he could get to second base, he had to clear the problem of first base. Third base was something that might take a lot of healing. But, God, she looked good in those jeans, with her little flat shoes on and a pretty red sweater that hugged her in all the right places. He wanted to touch her hair and move the one stray lock that always came away from her ponytail over her shoulder, but thought better of it.

"Want a glass of wine now?" He watched her move down the hall with a light, easy glide.

A shrug in response was all he received. He'd take that as a yes, for the moment.

"Want to sit downstairs while we wait up for Ahmad . . . maybe put on some oldies?"

"Okay," was all she said as she headed down the stairs toward the living room.

He worked fast. Right on her heels, he flipped off lights, only leaving on a couple to make the mood romantic. Then he bounded into the kitchen to find the wineglasses and retrieve the bottle he'd stashed in the fridge. He shoulda bought some flowers. When was the last time he'd done that? Man . . .

This fight wasn't blowing over like most of their little spats. Sure, Maxine was calm—but as if she'd surrendered and was marking time, like a convict. That was no way for man and wife to live.

"Here, baby," he said in a cheerful voice, extending a glass to her as he reentered the living room and flopped beside her on the sofa. "Ooops. Forgot the music," he added nervously, jumping up to switch on the stereo and shuffling through the CDs to find some of the Greatest Hits compilations that might make her remember why they'd gotten married in the first place.

Maxine studied the light pink liquid in the glass as she held it by the stem. Okay, she had been peaceable, gracious, had stopped the feud. She had done what she was supposed to do. She had taken care of every household need today, just like she did every day. But she had nothing to say to this man who was trying his best to get a make-up night going. She closed her eyes. Men just didn't get it, did they?

How was a woman, after being hurt to the bone, after having to literally fight with somebody to listen to her, supposed to suddenly flip the internal switch like Kenny was flipping on the stereo, and become some love goddess? He was a good man, a good father, a good provider . . . but she wanted him to be a good friend to her again. That was the oldie she missed, not merely the music. But she doubted that he'd give her the time to explain why that was so important now.

She took a sip of wine rather than say anything. He'd put on some stuff from the mid-eighties. Their era. Yeah, Kenny was reaching deep to pull a rabbit out of the hat.

"Listen, baby . . . ," Kenny began, all serious, talking low and sexy. "I know things between us have been a bit strained for the last couple of days. But you know I love you, right?"

She nodded but didn't smile. What has *that* got to do with it? She loved him, too. That aspect of the point was moot. Problem was, she didn't *like* him very much these days. "I love you, too," she said coolly, taking a sip of her wine and then studying the way the light shimmered inside the glass.

"Maxine, look at me," he said with a sigh, taking her glass from her and setting it down on the coffee table. She did, and he hesitated for a moment. "You can take the class with my blessing. Okay?"

She almost laughed as she stared back at him. He was doing it again—giving her permission, as though she were one of the children. Where was her life part-ner, her friend, in all of this?

"Thank you." Her response had come out more crisply than she'd intended, and she reached for her glass again, needing a shield between her mouth and his. She could tell he was angling to kiss her, and she was in no mood for that.

When his hand went to her thigh, she just glanced down at it and stared. He removed it immediately

"Baby . . . I miss you."

Yeah, I bet the hell you do, she thought as she took another careful sip from her glass. She eyed him as he reached for his wine and took a healthy swallow. That's right; back up until *I* give *you* permission. You don't own me, so don't put your hands on me! While her face remained placid, one-liners were zinging through her skull. This rage was so profound, down so deep, she could hardly explain it to her own mind, much less voice it.

And it went waaaay back—beginning with every sin-gle concept and idea that he'd squashed. She thought back to the first job she had to leave upon Kenny's insis-tence, because she was carrying Ahmad. Then she was pregnant with Kelly. Then the baby . . . And each time, in between carrying these children she loved with all her heart, she'd tried to find a little piece of space for herself, but Kenny had said it wasn't the right time, or was resistant. She hadn't been right since he'd made her feel worthless at Chadway Towing. And then he'd resisted her being in a political campaign. This time she would not allow him to strip the concept of writing from her.

She leaned her head against the sofa and closed her

eyes, listening to the music and hoping it would mitigate some of her anger. But her fingers were tightly clasped around the stem of her wineglass.

"Yeah, honey, like old times," he murmured, threading his arm behind her neck so it could drape over her shoulders. "Me, and you, and some music, and some wine, just relaxing at home. That's all we needed to get back to normal."

Normal? It took all her powers of self-control not to leap from the couch and strike him. Get back to normal? Maxine steadied her breathing and focused on the slow Luther Vandross ballad. Normal by the old definition meant doing things Kenneth Chadway's way without argument. It meant going along with his program and not rocking the boat with a program of her own. Normal is what got them here in the first place.

Memories crowded her brain as her husband began stroking her arm. Where had the butterflies gone? They used to invade the pit of her stomach when he did that. Just the anticipation alone had once been enough to make her giddy and excited about the evening's possibilities. Now she was sitting on the sofa wanting to throw Kenny's arm off her. She had to think, had to put all this anger into context. She wasn't even making sense to herself.

"Want some more wine?" He had asked the question against her neck, landing a light kiss on her collarbone.

"Yeah," she replied, her tone flat. Anything to get him off her and out of her personal space. His attention was making the hair stand up on the back of her neck, not sending shivers down her spine. Lord help her—what was wrong with her?

She watched him walk away toward the kitchen and issue a sly wink over his shoulder, thinking everything was all right. It wasn't. Things were broken like a fractured plate of china. One hairline crack, and then everything had fallen apart. But his retreat gave her space to think.

When did it begin to feel like this? From the outside, everybody thought they had the ideal household, marriage, and family. In many respects, they did. The kids were good, healthy, and respectful. That was a blessing. They weren't rich, but they weren't poor. *That* was a blessing. Her husband still looked good to her, too . . . He didn't cheat, didn't drink, didn't hit her. . . . He was a good father. They'd been lovers and friends since high school. So, what was wrong with her?

How could one little spat about a stupid class dredge up all this fury?

Friends, she thought, as Kenny returned with a smile and handed her the glass of wine. That was it. They weren't really friends anymore . . . but when did that happen? And why did that make her so angry? Why now?

"Thank you," she murmured, accepting the glass from him and taking a liberal sip.

He chuckled. "You'd better take it easy, Maxine, or you'll be looped before Ahmad gets home."

"Yeah," she murmured with a smile.

"Or maybe that could be a good thing? Hmmm?"

She watched him laugh and the way the corners of his eyes crinkled when he did. That was it. They didn't laugh together anymore. They only laughed about what made him laugh, only talked about what made him excited, expectant, happy. They used to laugh about what made them *both* happy . . . talk about what made them both worry.

He'd almost died in a car accident. Her sister had almost died in that same accident, and then Bird had been lucky not to have cancer. Why was she the only one noticing the shortness of time? Why was he content to fall into a rut, okay with the status quo, when they'd been spared? There were so many things to talk about, but he never wanted to explore the deep regions of her mind or heart . . . like he used to. Through it all, he'd never even asked her if she'd been scared—and she was. She'd been terrified.

Her finger traced the edge of her glass, and she could see him watching her from her peripheral vision. Yeah . . . it started back during his accident . . . when he stole the joy from her running the towing business while he was down. Until then, she hadn't realized that he never really considered her a partner, not even a helpmeet. Until then, she didn't know how much he resented her thriving and growing on her own—and that did something to her. Especially when he gave his female office manager more credit for keeping things running than he did her. And then the woman had the nerve to make a play for him, which he hid. Something got broken right then and there. The first crack.

Maxine sighed.

"Whatcha thinkin' about, baby?"

She shook her head. Her thoughts needed time to gel before she voiced them. "Just relaxing and listening to the music."

"Good," he murmured, and sat back and closed his eyes.

She was glad, because tears were fighting their way up toward her lashes. She thought about how she'd run for public office, and how he'd reacted to her attempt. It wasn't until the very end that he'd embraced the concept, but by then her feelings had been so wounded, he couldn't even fathom just how much. And like a flower killed by ice and storms, she just went underground and back to business as usual—a bulb, waiting for the warmth of spring to try to peek out again.

But that warmth never came. He wanted her to just do what she'd always done, and never bloom or grow. And when she started budding with her writing, and coming to him excited about it, he'd just grunted.

That's what she wanted to talk about tonight. Her writing. Each time he'd begrudgingly agreed to read a passage or a poem, all he would say was, "Maxine, that's nice." No dialogue. No, "Baby where did you get that idea?" No, "Wow, that was deep. You should lengthen it, make it into a short story." No encouragement to stretch, grow, or flower. Not even a chuckle about remembering those days she'd written about.

There was a time when he was her sun, and his rays of encouragement had brought out so much beauty in her. There was a time, too, when she felt like she was his sun. Now everything else was his light but her . . . even though she still gave him as much light as she could. Maxine nearly shook her head. Maybe she'd moved from being his sun to being his moon, revolving around him, waxing and waning, and only now having reflective light. . . . Had her own light really been dead for years?

After a silent struggle about her writing, he'd finally

taken a couple of her poems to bed with them to read—which was ultimately to his benefit, truth be told. It was an act done with resistance and heavy sighs of impatience—but she'd been so starved for any validation from him then that it had been enough. Now she needed more. She needed to know that he was solidly in her corner.

That's why she couldn't let the anger go. The prospect of living with this man for another seventeen years until their baby girl was grown, living with someone who wouldn't let her into his world at work, who didn't want her to have any interests beyond the house without his expressed approval, and only if it didn't inconvenience him . . . seventeen more years, longer than they'd been married, of living with someone who would never validate or take part in or get excited about anything she was interested in, were staring at her in the face now, as Kenny lifted his head, opened his eyes, and came near to plant a kiss on her mouth. *Seventeen more years like this.*

Maxine turned her head. It wasn't a thought, but an instant reflex.

"What's the matter?" Her husband's eyes searched hers frantically as he drew back, stunned.

"I can't do this. Not for seventeen more years."

"What, Maxine?" Kenny took her hand. "Baby, you're scaring me."

"I'm scaring myself, Kenny," she whispered, tears falling. "I can't do this," she said, shaking her head. "I'm not my mother."

"Baby, *what* are you talking about?"

"I don't know," she said on a thick swallow.

"Look . . . we can go out, do stuff. But I need to know what's wrong, so I can fix it."

"Kenny, you can't fix it, because it's the way you think. It's what's in your heart. When I was younger it didn't matter, because I felt invincible, like I had time. But now it does matter. I was blind to that."

"What? You think I'm cheating, or something? In my heart? Maxine, talk to me. What's in my heart?"

She sat down her wineglass and covered her face with her hands, breathing into them slowly before drawing them away.

"We don't laugh anymore."

He just stared at her for a moment. "We were just laughing a few minutes ago. I don't get it."

"Not like that. I mean really laugh, giggle, plan, *dream* together. You used to have such a generous spirit."

He was quiet and studying her. "It's about the computer, right? You're mad because I wanted to know how much it cost and didn't just say, 'Go ahead, regardless of the price,' right?"

"It has nothing to do with that, Kenny." She could feel her body going stiff with frustration. "Everything I've always brought to you as an idea, or anything I was excited about, you always resist, right out of hand. Then you try to convince me that I'm crazy, or don't need to waste my time with it. Or that if I do it anyway, you don't want to be bothered with it."

He didn't say a word, but looked away.

"Then," she pressed on, "while I'm doing whatever thing it is that makes me happy, you take no interest in it. I can't come to you all excited and say, 'Oooooh, Kenny, guess what just happened?' We used to be friends. I still do that for you, and we squeal in the kitchen late at night, or in bed, about *your* news—but never about *mine*. That's what this is about."

Maxine stood up and walked toward the kitchen with her glass. "You miss your lover and your wife, you said earlier." She turned, and waited.

"Yeah, I do," he told her in an honest reply.

"I miss my friend so much," she said. "I need that before a man can be my lover . . . I always have. That's how you got me, Kenny. You were my friend."

She turned to refill her glass with wine. Rather than going back to normal by ending this evening on sex, she was going to do something not so normal for her— get good and damned drunk. Maxine almost laughed out loud. Picture that. Her. Drunk. She could hear Teri, now, suggesting marriage counseling. Oh, yeah, right, and get Kenny to go? Pulease.

Or, maybe she should tell Pastor—so he, in his old-time religion, could tell her to just submit to her husband's every desire, since, as a woman, she really wasn't supposed to have any. Yeah. Right. Just obey and it'll get better, by and by. Or tell Bird, so her other sister could suggest something really crazy that would blow the roof off her home? Not.

This little problem she would keep to herself. It was manageable. Just a bitter pill to swallow, but then, she'd been so blessed in every other area, who was she to argue with God? Maxine filled her glass to the rim and slurped it down halfway in two huge gulps.

She could feel Kenny's presence in the kitchen doorway. Didn't he know she was having a little private wake? She'd just learned that their friendship had died, and that meant a lot of what they had had also died. The marriage was on life support, automatic pilot. She breathed; her heart beat, her necessary functions, were taken care of; but she didn't feel a thing. Maxine almost sobbed. Couldn't she at least bury the dead part of their relationship in peace? She wasn't even angry with him anymore—just tired.

"Maxine," he said, his voice filled with worry. "I've never seen you like this before . . . and I didn't buy a bottle of wine for you to stand in the kitchen and drain it like that. What you're doing is seriously concerning me, baby. You don't normally act like this."

She looked at him, took another sip, and shrugged. "I'm just burying the dead, Kenny. I have to get used to the fact that things have changed. You don't like me anymore—because I'm not a high school girl. I've grown up and I don't fit your mold of expectations. And I don't like you—because of how you treat me. Not bad, mind you, just . . . just . . ." She searched for the words that would not come as she grasped at the air with her hand, then gave up. "Doesn't matter."

His eyes spoke volumes. Alarm, anger, hurt, mostly confusion, registered in them and reflected back at her. She weaved a bit where she stood, and then polished off her glass of wine.

"I don't want to fight," she said, pouring another glass of wine. "Want one?"

"No. And, I don't want to fight either," he said in a whisper.

"Okay, then we agree on something."

"Maxine, put the wine down and come sit down on the sofa."

"And be a good girl," she sighed. "I will. Don't worry. We can probably still make up for Wednesday night after I've had a few more glasses of wine."

"You need a glass of wine to be with me now, Maxine?"

The hurt in his expression did something to her. Why was she trying to cut him with words? Maybe she just wanted him to feel what she was feeling, and to mourn and grieve the loss with her. Maybe she just needed him to really share something with her.

Or maybe she was afraid that he was right . . . perhaps she was dabbling, as he called it. What if she didn't have what it took to write the way she wanted to . . . the way she needed to in order to do justice to the stories? But then, a friend would encourage her to hone her skills so she could accomplish her cherished goal. Again, he didn't know what had frightened her—a friend would. Because a friend would have heard how important any one of these things had been and were to her. If he listened more . . .

Residual anger still lingered in her, and she needed him to at least validate that they were no longer friends, and not just blithely go along like nothing had happened—as if how she felt was foolish and didn't matter. Her tongue was becoming a carving knife, right there in her own kitchen, but she didn't have the will to stop herself. Her brain told her to say something to retract the nasty comment, but her mouth wouldn't form the words. They just stood there, husband and wife, looking at each other. She'd seen stuff like this on daytime talk shows—people caught in a standoff. She'd watched Dr. Phil make people deal with their problems on *Oprah,* and she'd listened while working and had shaken her head at those messed-up lives. And now here she was, getting wasted in her own kitchen with a good husband standing at the doorway practically wringing his hands. She had lost her mind.

Maxine laughed out loud. "Oh, Kenny, I'm sorry!" She doubled over and kept laughing. "Ooooh-weeee, I am crazy."

He just stared at her.

"I haven't had wine in ages . . . months, and months, and months."

"Maxine, come sit down. I'll make a pot of coffee. Ahmad shouldn't see you like this."

"You're right," she whispered, covering her mouth with her hand. "But." She burst out laughing. "You are going to fix me a cup of coffee?" Maxine held onto the edge of the sink, bent over it, and laughed harder through a torrent of tears nearing hysteria. "Oh, my Father in Heaven. The man is going to do coffee for me—thirteen years, and I get a cup of coffee! Seventeen more, and I might work my way up to breakfast in bed." She was wiping her eyes as she gulped in huge breaths of air and stood up straight. "Excuse me," she said, still chuckling and wiping her face. "Oooh, boy. That was a good one."

Kenny didn't say a word, but simply guided her to the sofa and deposited her with a thud, then gave her his back to consider as he strode from the living room to the kitchen. Oooops. She'd done it now. Had hurt his ego. Oh, well. But, her mind kept going over his question. "You need wine to be with me now, Maxine?"

Yeah. She did. She needed morphine to stop this level of hurt. When he came back in here, she'd tell him, too. Happened sorta slow, like the way termites eat a house from the inside out, and then one day the floor caves in, or a support beam breaks.

"Yup. Just like that," she said to the empty room, snapping her fingers while her eyes remained closed. "Thought it only happened to other people. Not us."

What about this didn't he understand, though? She was gonna tell him how it worked in the female mind. Now see, when he was so nasty about her help at the business, criticizing everything she did—she could take that, because that she could chalk up to pure male ego. She had invaded his space, plus he was injured. So that was forgivable. Made sense. "Yeah, made sense," she muttered into the nothingness. Then when that hussy employee of his tried to make a play for her man—well, that brought out the fight in her. Basic instinct, and it was all cool because she found out he didn't act upon the offer. All-righty now.

When she ran for office, she could sorta see his point—it would have been very chaotic around the Chadway ranch if she'd won, and he did come around at the end. Okay. Fine. But see, what he didn't understand was, even iron wears out—like Mama Joe's mama would say. That was Grandma's saying. Even iron wears out.

And there was no excuse for being so resistant about her writing, or being so begrudging about reading anything she wrote. Being a writer was the perfect career for a stay-at-home mother like herself. The hours were flexible, the work could be done from home, and like

Teri and Bird had said, if she was to ever really make it take off, she could substantially add to the family coffers—so what was his issue? Not to mention, it only caused a little temporary inconvenience to the household, not some major drama.

If Kenny was her friend, he would have rooted for her, been happy that she'd found something positive and life-affirming to do within the fabric of their family unit—something that could last for the children long after she was gone. But he didn't treat her like a friend. Why did a man always treat a woman like a lover and not a friend?

"Yup. Even iron wears out," she murmured against the music. Last Wednesday, Kenny had thrown the final pail of cold water on anything that had smoldered for him. Never before had she felt such nothingness at his touch. Nope. Never.

She had put "doing him" on her list like another chore today, she sadly admitted to herself as she curled up in a ball on the couch. Yup. Just like that—overnight. Squashed. No more romantic intent. All because he'd ceased to be her friend. In the past, there'd been times when he wanted some and she really wasn't up to it, but once they got going, she'd loved every minute of it.

A single fat tear slipped beneath her lids and rolled down the bridge of her nose. She didn't even bother to wipe it away. Because there were also times when she wanted to, and he'd been too tired. Come to think about it, why did it always work in the reverse? When he was too tired, she had to accept the situation, no matter how she felt. But when she was too tired, he pressed the issue and always got some. There was a lot of stuff around here that wasn't right, come to think about it.

"C'mon, baby. Sip this, and get yourself together."

She sat up and accepted the steaming mug of coffee. She peered into it. Black. After all these years, he should know how she took her coffee—light, with a lot of sugar.

"Kenny, what's my favorite color?"

"Oh, Maxine," he said with impatience. "Drink the damned coffee and pull yourself together."

"You don't remember, do you?" She stared at him, totally sobered by his inability to answer her. She stood, not a wobble in her balance. Her hands found her hips. "A good friend would know."

"I . . . Uh . . . Blue. Right?"

Maxine shook her head and brushed past him. That was it. She'd take a shower, brush her teeth, go to bed, and sleep with one eye opened until her son came safely home.

Wine was not the solution. Talking to Kenny wasn't the solution. There was only one thing to do: get herself together.

five

a mild headache had been Maxine's constant companion all morning, but she had things to do. She glanced up from her yellow legal pad and brought the button of her pen to her lips to think as she watched Kelly follow the ballet teacher's instructions. Soft classical music filtered behind the teacher's commands.

"And one, and two, and up on our toes, ladies."

The little girls all looked so cute in their pink leotards, with their S-shaped bodies, fat little bellies, high round behinds, and no woman form to them yet. Maxine chuckled, the image of them doing pirouettes holding her headache temporarily at bay.

Her baby girl was in a gymboree class downstairs in the community center, which would last another half hour, and Ahmad was no problem. Basketball had him for two hours at least, and then he'd be off to get a burger with some friends. She smiled.

The evening before was now just vapor, ephemeral, nothing to hold onto. Husbands and wives had disagreements all the time. The main thing was that she'd gotten herself together. Two days and two nights of dwelling on the negative had been an indulgence. Now it was time to get to work.

Scribbling with determination, she continued to draft her prose. Tonight she'd type it into her new laptop; she wasn't yet familiar enough with it to tote it with her during her day. She chuckled to herself. Or sophisticated enough at this point to just pop it open in public and use it like she'd seen other affluent urban professionals use theirs. One day. For now, she'd do it the old-fashioned way.

The thought of old-fashioned ways drew her back to the page. She wanted to have something good to take to class with her. The flyer had said it would be a work-in-progress seminar, a place where would-be writers could polish their work. She was not about to show up to Paul Gotier's class with a raggedy old journal of scattered thoughts and her diary from yesteryear. No way.

So after the kids were finished, she'd run the other errands on her list, hit the supermarket, get home and put the food away, call her sisters to check on what to bring for Sunday dinner, and then resume her writing. She could do this, Kenny's vibe notwithstanding. All she had to do was remain pleasant, keep her routine, and ignore any negativity he cast in her direction.

If she were lucky, she might even be able to hook up with some fellow writers in the class, and then she'd have some people to share her passages with, to bounce ideas off and brainstorm with. Just because her husband wasn't interested in her particular endeavor would not be the end of the world. Couples often had different interests. That would have to be fine.

But a pang of wistfulness entered her chest at the

thought. Kenny didn't have to be a writer or a literature buff, just like she didn't have to be a bowling or fishing or football enthusiast. However, it would have been nice if he'd been a cheerleader of sorts, recognizing that this was something she truly enjoyed. That alone should have been enough. Just like she provided munchies for his football extravaganzas with his buddies, occasionally went down to the bowling alley, or made a big fuss over some new rod-and-tackle get-up he'd bought.

Maxine sighed and banished the thought. No sense in dwelling on what could be, especially when she had so much to do.

He'd spent all day trying to avoid this woman he no longer knew. On Saturdays, it was easy to do that. Yard work, going down to the garage to get his weekend crew on the ball, and taking his son to his various activities always filled his day. Plus Maxine was perpetually a blur of errands and activity on a Saturday, so he didn't have to come up with excuses to stay out of her path. It was Saturday night that was going to be a problem.

Maybe tonight he'd hook up with his boys. Maybe Lem could get out on a furlough pass, or he could find a running buddy to grab a beer and go hear some jazz or something, since Maxine was ignoring him, typing away at that blasted new computer. And what was that about, anyway? She'd acted like a lunatic, not making any sense. She had gotten looped, and was laughing and crying, and then had just gone upstairs and went to sleep like it was nothing. Then she had the nerve to wake up all cheerful and start her day like nothing out of the ordinary had happened. She didn't even say anything about his offer to take her to dinner. Probably didn't even remember he'd asked her, anyway. He wasn't buying wine again. *Ever.*

Yeah. He was going out. And he would stay out and come back when he felt like it, since nobody seemed to notice him in his own house. *He* might even tie one on. *He* might even be the one to come home leaning to the side, and enter the house laughing and crying and acting simple. How would *she* like it then, if *he* was the one to ruin one of the nights they usually made love?

Kenny grabbed the phone and punched in Lem's number. He waited with impatience as the telephone rang several times before anyone picked it up.

"Hello?" Lem muttered, sounding winded and distracted.

Kenny paused for a second, then forced his salutation to be upbeat.

"Yo, Lem. What's up, brother?"

There was a hesitation before Lem spoke again.

"Oh, hey, Kenny. Uh . . . everything all right down at the garage?"

The question irritated him. True, he didn't generally call anybody, but why did the call have to be business related?

"Yeah, brother-in-law. Everything down there is fine."

"Good. Good," Lem said quickly before Kenny could say anything else. "Uh, look. Can I call you back? Uh . . . this isn't a good time."

He heard Bird giggle in the background. Kenny sighed and looked at his watch. Nine o'clock on a Saturday night, no teenagers in the house to stay up all hours and interrupt things. Yeah, his boy was *busy*. Like *he* should have been busy.

"Cool. I'll catch you later." Kenny hung up without even waiting for Lem to respond. Phone had probably dropped to the floor, anyway.

He walked through the house toward the kitchen and stood in the doorway, watching Maxine. She was totally focused on that damned computer. It grated him, how it absorbed her. She even had the nerve to be sitting there all serene, freshly showered, wearing one of his favorite robes, skin looking like brown butter—ignoring him.

"I'm going out," he announced.

"Okay," she replied in a pleasant tone.

"I don't know what time I'll be back."

"Okay," she murmured, sounding distracted and like she could care less.

"Might be real late, so don't wait up."

"No problem. Ahmad is sleeping over his friend's house. The boys are going to a morning basketball tournament with his friend's dad early tomorrow."

"Oh," he pronounced, needing something to latch onto, "so when did *this* get sanctioned? Maybe I might have wanted to take my own son to a game, or something."

"Friday at dinner when the boy asked you, and you said fine. Remember? That's when it got *sanctioned.*"

She hadn't even looked up at him, her fingers steadily clicking away. So Kelly was in bed, the baby was asleep, Ahmad was gone for the night, and his wife had the nerve to be sitting in the kitchen typing?

"So when were you going to remind me, huh?"

"Kenny," she said on a too-patient-sounding sigh.

"The boy asked, you said yes, he was all excited to go, and I didn't think it warranted any further discussion. You said you were going out, so why don't you do that?"

Oh, so now she was putting him out of his own house, was that it?

"You didn't think it warranted further discussion to remind me of where my son would be?"

He waited. He needed her to look at him. Wanted her to connect with him just once, and to stop this silly game of hers.

"No," she replied, flipping a page on her pad. "I really didn't, because you should know that I wouldn't allow a child of mine to be somewhere that wasn't safe, and where he hadn't already received permission to go."

Her statement was logical, patient, and it got on his damned nerves.

"Well, fine. I'm going out."

"Have a nice time. Drive safe."

Why was it that when a brother needed his boys, they were all on lockdown at home? Why was that, he wondered, staring into his beer. He glanced at the clock. It had only been an hour. He felt like time was playing games with him. He didn't feel like sitting on a barstool alone. There wasn't even a good game on that would burn up two or three hours. But he was gonna stay out till the bars closed, or bust.

Kenny looked around the familiar neighborhood establishment. Couples had come in together. Small groups of what he assumed to be friends gathered. Some people had hooked up with dates, or possibly one-nighters, while he sat by himself. He and Maxine should have been somewhere together. And what if some chick walked up to him and sat by him? What then? What if he bought some fine sister a drink and made small talk?

He cast another glance around the room and unfortunately caught the eye of a hard-looking woman who was at a table with two of her girlfriends. She smiled at him and offered a sexy wink—which wasn't the least bit sexy coming from her. Kenny immediately looked down into his beer and almost groaned out loud. Damn. All he could catch was an old barfly these days?

None of the women sitting there could hold a candle to his wife, even if he was that type of man—but he wasn't. He was blessed. Had a nice home, good family, decent business. Maybe it was just a change of seasons. Maxine was going through some little woman thing, and it would blow over soon enough. Wasn't about seriously rocking the boat, when she'd just pissed him off a bit.

Kenny polished off his beer and motioned for another one. He would just sit there, watch the end of the boring game he could care less about, and get his head right. Maybe by the time he got home, she'd be in bed. Then they could solve it all. He'd snuggle up to her, she'd chuckle and slide back against him, and it would all be over. Things would go back to normal, and in the morning she'd fix him a big breakfast before she went to church—like normal. He could do some work around the house and get ready for the dinner they'd have at Lem's. He'd be all relaxed and smiling like his brother-in-law, and it would be cool. Normal again.

When the bartender slid a refill his way, he nodded and brought the foaming mug to his lips. But Maxine had said some pretty harsh words—tipsy or not. Talking crazy about him not being her friend anymore. What did that mean? Hell, he was her husband, not some friend. Maxine needed to stop watching daytime TV, it was messing her mind up.

Before, if she got tipsy with him, it would be an incredible evening. "Damn," Kenny murmured into his glass. It had been a long time since Maxine had reacted so passionately in his arms. Maybe he was getting old, and losing his touch?

The thought sent an uncomfortable shiver through him. When she'd said he was no longer her friend, that had hurt. Cut him to the bone, because they were always the best of friends. He'd told her things that no other living soul knew. She had no idea how much he missed her. Not just being with her, but sitting on the sofa, laughing, or discussing some problem. He'd wanted to tell her all about how the paperwork on this new contract was kicking his ass—how the cash flow coming from the city was always a problem. Maxine was good with working out things like that.

She'd know what to do about the fact that they had to make the tows, then submit the hours in an invoice, and wait nearly ninety days for the city to get a check to his office, and how it meant he had to figure out how to pay his men in the interim—because a working guy couldn't wait ninety days to feed his family. None of the guys would stay with him if he did business like that. Then that caused a drain on his bills, too. His utilities had to be paid at the business and the house. The trucks needed gas, maintenance, repairs. . . . There were important issues he needed to bounce off Maxine.

By the time Kenny looked up, his glass was nearly empty. He glanced at the clock again, and noted only another half hour had passed. Out for an hour and a half, and he was ready to go home. He shook his head. Yeah, he must be getting old. There was a time when he could have hung out all night, come home with the sun, and still put in a full day at the garage. Now look at him.

He motioned for another beer, even though the mug he held still had something in it.

"Think you need to slow down, boss?" The bartender gave him an appraising look.

Kenny shrugged.

"How about if I bring you another one in a few—after you finish that one, my man?"

Kenny let his breath out hard and downed the rest of the beer in his mug. "Whatever."

It took a minute, but he got the key in the front door and turned the locks. As expected, the house was quiet. Common sense was starting to ease its way back into his head—he was gonna pay for this in the morning. It had been ages since he done this; he hated the way the morning after felt. This was all Maxine's fault.

Kenny swayed a little as he made his way to the coat hooks and, with a bit of difficulty, removed his jacket and hat. All he had to do was get up the stairs and make it to the bed. He counted his footsteps, watching them as he advanced toward the stairs, ensuring that he didn't bump into anything. Okay, he told himself as he got to the top of the landing, just walk the line down the hallway, open the bedroom door nice and slow, and the bed will be in reach.

Steadying himself, he made it inside the room. Maxine was resting, her back to his side of the bed, and moonlight washed her in a silver aura. God, she was pretty. Oh, yeah, he almost forgot. They weren't speaking. It was her fault, and she had the nerve to be lying there all sexy, and what not. Wasn't fair to string a man out like that and then be all sexy. Just wasn't right.

He stooped to unlace his boots, wobbled, and sat down hard on the side of the bed. Maxine stirred and opened her eyes, and he studied her face. The expression on it was calm. She wasn't angry. Then she pulled the covers up over her shoulders, sighed hard, and closed her eyes again. All right. Good. She wasn't going to start in on him.

Stripping down to his shorts, leaving everything in a pile on the floor, he clumsily slid into bed. He hadn't planned to do it, but by reflex, he found himself spooning her. God, she smelled good . . . like that cocoa butter stuff she wore . . . or was it shea butter? Whatever. She felt like it, too, and it smelled good and felt good.

"You 'sleep?" he murmured against her hair.

"I *was* asleep," she answered in a weary voice.

Good, she was awake. He breathed in her scent again, feeling it thread through his system and pulse in his groin.

"You smell so good, baby. . . ."

"You smell like a bar," she returned flatly. "Good night, Kenny."

Just like that. How could she do that to him?

"I miss you, baby—"

"You know what?"

Maxine pulled away so fast that it was almost sobering. She sat up and clicked on the light, practically blinding him. He shielded his eyes with his forearm. Damn, not now, not an argument in this condition.

"I was in here minding my business, asleep, Kenneth. And you come in here drunk, trying to get some? Are you crazy!"

Guilty as charged. He had to be out of his mind. Only a fool would come in and wake his wife, drunk, expecting her to roll over and give him some. But she could have had a little mercy, knowing that he was loose, and it had been a while. He was angry, but he didn't say a word. Hell, he was no match for her verbally when sober, let alone drunk and amorous. He needed to go to sleep before the room started spinning.

"You know how many nights I just complied, because you wanted to? Coming in all funky from wherever? And now, I'm supposed to be ready—just because you are, huh? Is that it? Well, think again. I might like to be asked out to dinner, *nicely.* Invited, *not commanded,* like I had to put a gun to your head to get taken out on a date! And if you think I'm going to just take that type of treatment for another seventeen years, you've got another thing coming, buddy. Do I make myself clear, Kenneth?"

She didn't even seem to draw a breath as her words sent machine-gun-rapid fire into his brain. He couldn't even get a round off. Seventeen years? What was she talking about? Did he miss some anniversaries, or something? They hadn't been married that long. Damn, he was drunk. "Maxine, seventeen—"

"That's right. Seventeen years more to go, and I'm not taking this from you. So don't you be sliding in here smelling like a brewery and trying to jump on me. You might not have any interest in my writing, or the things that interest me, or think I do anything all day long, but I work hard, too. And I want to be treated with a little consideration and appreciation from time to time. So you just roll your drunk behind over on your side of the bed and sleep it off, 'cause you aren't touching me tonight."

Oh, God. The room was spinning, and she was ragging so fast, bits of her sentences were hard to catch. Before he could open his mouth, the light went off, her body stiffened, the cover was snatched from his side of the bed to hers, and the storm went still.

Damn. A brother didn't stand a chance.

Daylight stabbed him in the eyes through his shut lids. No breakfast smells wafted through the house. Kenny pulled himself to the side of the bed and hung his throbbing head. Carefully, and very slowly, he pulled himself off the edge of the bed and made it down the hall, holding onto the wall for support. Finally able to stop swaying while taking a leak, he figured that Maxine had already gone to church. What time was it, anyway?

He could only pray that the Lord would be his salvation. Maybe in church, some Christian forgiveness would enter her soul, or might rub off from some of the saved onto her to also save him. Maybe at her sister's house this afternoon she'd return to being pleasant, and he could eat with some laughter around him.

The morning after was a bitch.

* * *

"So, Max, have you gotten the hang of your new computer yet?"

Kenny didn't make eye contact with Lem as Bird cheerfully asked the question. Since his wife hadn't spoken to him all day, and going to church hadn't changed anything, he just passed the bowl of collard greens that Bird had thrust in his direction on to Teri.

Maxine chuckled and wiped the baby's mouth. "I've got it all loaded, Bird. Took me a while, but I'm cooking with natural gas on it now."

"I am so proud of you, Maxine," Teri said, speaking to her sister but looking in Kenny's direction. "We're *all* proud that you are taking that writing class next week, and we are *all* here to *fully* support you in your efforts."

Teri was starting. Heaven help him. Kenny just put a shovel full of macaroni and cheese in his mouth. *C'mon, Lem, how about a little backup?*

"Yeah," Ahmad added, "Mom is really good. I showed her how to get the Internet working, and how to use the little plug to put into the wall in the phone line if she needs to do research. That laptop is da bomb."

A strained silence fell for a moment.

Ahmad glanced between his mom and dad, wondering whether or not the rest of the family had noticed the tension. It was happening all over again, just like it did when his father was hurt in the accident. On the one hand, he could see his mother's point, yet he also knew his dad always acted weird when he was worried . . . maybe even a little afraid. It wasn't that his dad was against her, but he was probably feeling pretty bad about not being as book-smart as Mom. Plus,

Mom was always good at things like homework and computers—something his dad had never been good at. Just like she was good at handling the paperwork. His father had cut a glare at him. Yeah, Dad was scared. That had to be it.

Kenny tore his gaze from Ahmad and studied his plate. Now they had made his own son a coconspirator.

"Good for you, Ahmad," Teri finally said. "That is so nice that your mom is getting the support she needs *at home* from *her family.*"

Ahmad swallowed a sigh. *Aunt Teri, please don't start, Dad just can't take it today.*

"Uhmmm-hmmm," Bird muttered. "I know what it's like to start something new and just need *some encouragement.* So you go, Maxine. Don't let *nothing* get in your way, girl."

Ahmad looked down at his plate. If Aunt Teri *and* Aunt Bird were on Dad's case, then his dad didn't stand a chance. If Mama Joe were alive, she would have been able to tip the balance a little more fairly. She always knew what to say to make everybody feel needed and loved. Ahmad looked up at his Uncle Lem with a furtive glance. *Somebody do something!*

Kenny glimpsed his brother-in-law from the corner of his eye. He was on his own. Lem wasn't trying to rock his own boat by helping him out. His boy had just left him hanging out there.

"Mommy said she's writing things about Grandma," Kelly giggled, "so one day we'll all be able to remember Mama Joe. I never got to meet her, like Ahmad."

"And I bet Mom is also gonna write about how Dad and Mama Joe were so close, and about all the good stuff Dad did to help her around the house when she was alive, ya know?" Ahmad kept his eyes trained on his father, who ignored him with a grunt, and then watched his mother's expression. She never looked up. This was bad.

"You're writing about Mama Joe?" Bird squealed. "Oh, Maxine, that's wonderful." She leaned over and kissed Maxine, and caught little Jay's hand before he could fling any greens off his plate.

None of them were getting it. Ahmad let his breath out in a quiet rush. It was gonna get worse around their house before it got better.

"Yeah," Maxine said with a sigh. "There are so many good times we had around this house, and her recipes . . ."

"Oh, Max, that's fabulous. We have a family griot!" Teri reached over to cover Maxine's hand with her own. "I can't wait to read what you've written."

Kenny glanced at his wife between forkfuls of food. The sparkle had returned to her eyes for her sisters, and while she was chatting about this writing stuff. A tinge of something akin to jealousy went through him. Used to be a time when he created that look on her face. Whatever.

Maxine was shaking her head and chuckling softly. "It'll be a while before it's ready for anybody to read. I'm just glad I was able to get into that class with Paul Gotier."

Ahmad froze, his fork in midair.

"Paul Gotier?" Teri's tone forced Kenny to look up. "You never said it was a *Gotier* class!"

Who the hell was Paul Gotier? Kenny glanced at

Lem for clarification, but his brother-in-law seemed as clueless as he did. Kenny glanced at his son, who had shoved food in his mouth and looked down.

"Yeah," Maxine was saying with a wry smile. "He comes to town annually to give back to the community."

"Max!" Bird had nearly levitated out of her chair. "Oh, Max!"

Kenny knew better than to say a word.

Ahmad tried to keep from choking with a sip of iced tea.

Lem pushed food around on his plate.

"I know," Maxine sighed. "I was so lucky. His classes are limited, and usually before anybody really finds out he's coming, the class is filled. Just by happenstance, I was in the library when they were putting up the flyer and registration list. I can't believe it myself."

"How fortunate," Kenny grumbled against his better judgment.

"Oh, Maxine," Teri said with a twinkle in her eyes. "You are going to have the chance to learn from the best of the best."

"I know," Bird practically swooned. "His work is fabulous." She turned to Teri, and the three women shared a private giggle. "Did you read his second book?"

"Oooooh, Bird. Don't even talk about it," Teri exclaimed, fanning herself like it was hot in the room.

Again, Ahmad's glances darted between his parents' expressions. His father's worst fears were coming true—that some smart guy would steal Mom away. His dad had never said it, but a guy could tell what was on another guy's mind. It was all in how his father got tensed up when his mother knew something he didn't.

But that was so crazy. Mom was Mom; she wasn't going anywhere.

"That passage about—"

"Bird, don't even go there," Maxine laughed. "I won't be able to sit in class if I think about that." Then, as though catching herself, she nervously lowered her gaze and heaped more food on Ahmad's plate.

Ahmad just stared at his mother. She was acting all silly and dreamy about some guy . . . maybe Dad did need to worry. Maybe they all needed to worry.

Kenny watched his wife swallow away a smile. He didn't like this *at all.*

"Well, if he's a good writer, then maybe y'all should enlighten the unenlightened," Kenny said sullenly, wanting to leave the table.

"A good writer?"

The statement had come out as a chorus amongst the Joseph women. They looked at each other, burst out laughing, and shook their heads.

Even Lem stopped eating and glanced at his wife.

Ahmad's gaze shot between his father and his uncle. Yeah, older women had a thing about intelligent men— he knew that from the emphasis they put on good grades and homework—but he'd never seen his mom and aunts act like this about some guy.

"Who's Paul Gotier, Bird?"

Kenny folded his arms over his chest, satisfied by Lem's question and suspicious tone. Even his son was no longer in the female camp—he could tell by the way Ahmad had put down his fork to stare at his mother. Finally, some backup. This was dangerous, and he'd finally airlifted in some ammo.

"Lem, baby, Paul Gotier is the *sexiest,* most eligible, fine, poet, playwright, and novelist on the planet. I'll read you some of his passages . . . one night," she giggled, blushing.

Kenny groaned. Aw, man, now look at Lem. Sitting there like the Cheshire cat, totally disarmed at the promise of getting some good nookie when there was a serious issue on the table. Young bucks were so easily distracted from the matters at hand. Even his son looked disappointed in his uncle, because the boy just shook his head and started eating again.

Ahmad reached for a biscuit. *Mama Joe, you're gonna have to do something about this one. Everybody is crazy in here.*

"I heard his wife left him," Teri said in a conspiratorial tone. "I could *not* believe that when I read it in *Essence.* He talked about how going through that pain was embedded in his work, added texture that he didn't have there before."

"He didn't need more texture," Bird said, now laughing harder.

Maxine slapped her five, which irked Kenny.

Ahmad stared at his mom. That was uncool. That's the kinda stuff the girls at school did. Poor Dad . . . in front of the whole family, too!

"Well, if the man's wife left him, then I guess *Mr. Perfect* has some issues he's dealing with." Kenny picked up his fork and began to eat again, very satisfied when his son gave him a subtle nod of support.

"Oh, please, Kenny," Teri argued, defending this mystery man. "His wife was on drugs and left him to go into rehab. She left him with two little kids, who he's raising himself—as well as doing all his other literary and artistic projects. I'm impressed that he's still doing so much for the community."

"He's raising those two little kids all by himself?" Bird was wide-eyed. "Well, you've gotta respect that."

Lem stepped in. "Well, if I had his money, I could hire a housekeeper and baby-sitter and a cook and a maid and whatnot, Bird. Y'all have to put it all into perspective."

"Yeah," Ahmad added. "Money can make anybody seem like anything."

"That's right. That's right," Kenny chimed in. He pounded his son's fist. Even a teenager could see what was real versus fake.

"Wrong," the chorus sounded again.

"According to his interview," Teri corrected, "the man said he wanted his children to be raised with a sense of community, and not to be raised as spoiled wealthy children without ambition." Teri glanced around to receive her sisters' nods. "So he cooks, has no formal maid—just a little help once a week, which any working person could use—and takes them with him while touring. Frankly, I applaud the man, because he could have just left them with his mother in St. Lucia."

Appearing triumphant, Teri cast a disparaging glance toward the men at the table and then returned her focus to Maxine. "Anyway, literary great Alice Walker said, 'No person is your friend who demands your silence or denies your right to grow.' So I can only assume that anyone who is a loving family member or a friend would be happy for you to have this opportunity, Maxine."

It was more than his nerves could bear, and Kenny blasted a rebuttal toward his sister-in-law.

"Yeah, Teri, say what you want to say, but can the man drop a transmission in? Huh? Can he lay concrete, fix a fence, wire a house, do plumbing, or anything of *real* use around a house? Probably why his wife started taking drugs in the first place!"

Kenny glanced at Lem and then his son and received an even nod from both of them. "Women don't want a soft man. They want somebody who can do something with his hands, not just type on a dumb keyboard."

Now he was finished. Had said his piece and said it well. The Joseph women sat there, mouths open. Vindicated, Kenny leaned back in his chair and gave Teri, and then Maxine, the eye. But why were Lem and Ahmad looking down at their plates?

Ahmad sighed. His father was in too deep to be helped. This was the sort of thing that always sent Mom ballistic—and now he'd embarrassed her in front of her sisters. Things were gonna be bad around the house for a long time.

"Kenneth Chadway, I cannot believe you just said that." Bird was sputtering as she spoke. "First of all, nobody can make another person go on drugs. You aren't making a bit of sense. Second of all, how is typing on a keyboard dumb? Is Ahmad doing his homework dumb? If so, then why are you so hell-bent on making your own son do well in his academics, huh?"

Ahmad couldn't even look up as his father stammered and got cut off by his aunt Bird. Yeah, this was real bad.

"And third of all," Bird fussed, "Paul Gotier might or

might not be able to do all the stuff you said; we don't know the man. But I'll tell you this, you'd better stop talking about those things being the only *real* work a person does, and stop invalidating the other things."

Bird folded her arms over her chest, which was heaving with fury. Kenny'd seen Maxine puff up like that enough to know it when he saw it. Teri was clutching her iced tea glass so tightly, he was sure she'd crack it in her hands.

"So, Kenneth, do you mean to say that if you aren't doing drywall or fixing the fence or taking out the trash, you aren't doing man's work, which means you must be doing women's work—which is not as hard, or serious, or valuable? Tell me you did not just sit here at this table and go there." Teri shook her head. "Lord have mercy, Maxine *Joseph* Chadway, how do you put up with him?"

Kenny glanced at his wife, who was holding a fork in midair. Even the children had stopped eating and were looking at him. Lem was chewing a biscuit, trying to lie low. Ahmad was staring a hole in his plate.

"See, y'all read more into what I was saying than what I said. Everybody's been so touchy lately. All I was saying was that—"

"That there is no value in anything other than the things you know how to do. Ladies, let it go, and don't even argue with him. I don't anymore," Maxine cut in, dismissing him. "Water off a duck's back. Let it roll."

"Let it roll?" Teri had folded her arms over her chest now, and she glanced at Bird. "Show him the picture in the magazine, Bird. Show him how *soft* Paul Gotier is. Humph!"

"Bird," Lem warned, "don't do it. Let's just all chill and eat dinner. I'm sure Kenny didn't mean any harm, and the feathers are flying now for no reason."

Kenny cast a glance of appreciation for his support in Lem's direction. Now his son was looking at his aunt, sending a silent plea that anyone with common sense could read.

"Oh, no," Bird protested. "I have the magazine." She was on her feet before Lem could stop her. "Treating my sister like she's losing her mind because she wants to take a class . . . hmmmph."

That did it. Now he was hot. It was one thing to know that he'd been discussed; it was purely another thing to have his nose rubbed in it. Kenny flung his napkin on the table.

"I don't need to see no damned magazine, Bird. In fact, I'm through eating and talking about any of this."

"Aw, now see, Bird," Lem soothed, following his wife into the other room to stop her from bringing the dreaded article into the room. He paused mid-archway and turned to Kenny. "Brother-in-law, you know how Bird is. Now you just stay put, relax, everything is cool." His head turning again, Lem hollered, "Bird!" Then he was gone.

Maxine smoothed the front of her dress and expelled a breath of exasperation. Teri was grumbling to herself about not being able to believe all the drama. The children, wide-eyed, glanced from adult to adult but continued to eat. Kenny felt like his head was going to explode. Ahmad looked away again, as though to preserve what was left of his father's dignity. *In front of his own son.* The nerve! Finally Bird came back to the table without a magazine in her hand, fussing all the way at Lem and asking him, "What do you mean, You know how Bird is?"

Kenny felt bad for Lem, who was now in the doghouse on his account.

"So, how am I, Lem?" Bird had both hands on her hips.

"Baby," Lem stuttered, "uh, look . . . I didn't mean anything by it."

Trying to help out, Kenny ventured to step in. "Bird, he didn't mean anything really. We all flew off the handle on some rhetorical issue—who cares who this guy is, what he does, whatever. Right? He's not in our family. So let's all squash this nonsense and finish eating."

Bird sat down slowly, as did Lem, but all eyes were on Maxine. Although Kenny had focused on his plate, he could still see his wife from the corner of his eye. She was eating, but just barely. For a long time, no one said a word. Well, that was just fine by him. If they would all just eat and not talk, that was just fine.

Ahmad studied the group from a remote place in his mind. Why did the adults in the family always have some drama going on? Things would be cool for a while, then all of a sudden something would flare up. Things were different when Mama Joe was alive.

As soon as the kids went to bed and he'd been able to corner Maxine alone in their own kitchen, Kenny let her have a piece of his mind.

"Maxine, I don't know how you could go to your sisters with our business like that—telling them I'm unsupportive, or whatever it is that you said."

She gave him her back to talk to as she prepared lunches for Monday morning, and issued an impatient sigh.

"Kenny, you already said your piece at Sunday dinner, and I'm really in no mood to get into some unnecessary dispute."

"Seems like you haven't been in the mood for a lot of things, lately." He folded his arms in front of him and glared at her. What was she going to say to that? Humph!

Maxine sucked her teeth, but didn't look up. "And I wonder why."

Her tone was so blasé that it worked its way under his skin, right into his bloodstream.

"You tell your sisters that part of the thing, too?"

"No," she grumbled, sounding thoroughly disgusted. "Your secret is safe with me."

"My secret? My secret!"

"Please, Kenny. Stop yelling. You'll wake up the kids. I didn't say anything like that to them; you oughta know me better than that."

"I don't know *what* I know anymore, Maxine."

He wished that that would have at least made her look at him or raise her voice, or would have drawn some fire out of her. He was ready for a good old-fashioned yelling fest to clear the air. Instead, she simply shook her head as though she were dealing with one of the kids. It grated on him no end. She was so calm, and it was obvious that she'd gotten really good at letting anything he said or felt or did roll off her back. Maybe she really *didn't* care anymore. Hell, maybe he should have let Bird fetch that magazine so he could see what he was up against. A black Superman, to hear the ladies tell it. Some brother from another planet. Undercover brother—from some island, no less . . . the same kinda place Stella got her groove back. Aw, hell no, his wife wasn't taking that class.

"Maxine, you need to seriously think about the chaos and havoc you are wreaking upon this family with this class and the whole writing escapade. This isn't the right time to be gallivanting off in the streets at night to—"

"*What?*"

Oh, boy, now he had her full attention, and she was looking at him, but not the way he'd intended.

"Kenneth Chadway, did I hear you right? *Gallivanting* in the *streets?* Escapade? Have you lost your mind?"

"Uh . . ."

"Apparently you have."

He watched her slap bread and meat together like he was sure she probably wanted to slap his face. Her tone was so sharp, he almost felt his throat to see if he'd been cut.

"All right, maybe gallivanting was an overstatement. But dammit, Maxine, you know what I mean."

"No, I don't know what you mean," she whispered. "I do not know who I am living with—or what era this household was transported back to, like a *Twilight Zone* episode. Lord give me strength." Maxine walked back and forth between the refrigerator and the table as though she was an emergency room nurse, chanting prayers On High the entire time.

If his wife was pacing and praying, he knew he had only one option: get out of her way.

six

It wasn't possible for Maxine to stay angry with Kenny. Waiting to take her class gave her that same tingly, excited feeling she used to get as a kid on Christmas Eve. When she got up on Monday morning, she almost had to pinch herself to be sure that it wasn't a dream, that she only had a couple of days before she'd be doing something she'd always wanted to do. By Wednesday, sitting in Bird's salon chair, she couldn't keep the smile off her face.

"So, Miss Maxine, we're going to get you all ready for your first day at school." Bird giggled. "We're gonna get those huge pores under control with a nice facial, beat the calluses off your feet, do your nails, wax those bushy eyebrows, and wash and condition and tighten those locks—'all natural' still requires maintenance."

"Aw, Bird, I don't need all of that," Maxine argued, watching her toddler get passed from cooing hairdresser to cooing hairdresser. "My feet will be under shoes and socks, okay? So—"

"Oh, be quiet and sit back, Max," Bird insisted with

a loving push. "Let somebody pamper you for a change, would ya, sis?"

Laughing, Maxine relented, and soon she spied Teri coming through the door with shopping bags.

"Hi, ladies, Max," Teri announced, breezing through the door and making a beeline to Bird's salon chair. "Just picked up a little something for the family literary prodigy."

"What did you go and do, Teri?" Maxine kissed her sister as she plopped a big, glossy shopping bag on her lap.

Teri and Bird exchanged a wink. "Look for yourself," Teri replied, grinning.

Both of her sisters were practically giggling with excitement. Maxine reached down into the bag and produced a hard, square object wrapped in pink tissue. As she unfolded the paper, her hands slid against a buttery-feeling leather binder. The dark maroon, one-inch-thick portfolio had a zippered closure, and for a moment she could only stare at it.

"Oh, my God, Teri. What did you do?"

"Well, silly, you need to walk professionally through that door to claim your rightful place among the other writers. You can't go in there with Kelly and Ahmad's school supplies in a grocery store plastic bag, can you? This way, you can stow your writing pads, pens, etcetera, in one neat location."

Before Maxine could say a word, Bird had snatched the portfolio from her hands.

"It's a Coach!"

Within seconds the other stylists had come over to inspect it, each issuing affirmative sighs and comments.

"This is beautiful," Bird whispered in a reverent

tone. She opened it up and held it out for Maxine to inspect. "It's got new Cartier pens in there with matching pencils, and everything. Little section for business cards and whatnot. Oh, man, Teri, you've outdone yourself. Might make me go back to school, if you're handing out gifts like this."

"You can buy your own, Bird," Teri teased, taking the portfolio from Bird. "This is Maxine's—and Max, don't you let her try to so-called borrow it, you hear me? Bird never returns what she borrows, and this is for your writing. Okay?"

Tears had risen in Maxine's eyes, and she was on her feet now, hugging Teri while clutching the portfolio to her chest. "Nope, Bird," she chuckled through her tears of joy. "My big sister bought this for me, and you can't borrow it."

"Oh, silly, don't cry. But look in the little business-card section."

All the women converged on the chair to hover over Maxine's shoulder. When she flipped up the leather flap of the tiny compartment, the salon broke out in a collective "Oooohhhh . . ."

Her sister had made up mock business cards that read, "Maxine J. Chadway, author," with her street address, telephone number, and e-mail address on gorgeous linen stationery with a little quill-pen-and-bottle-of-ink logo next to her name.

Bird gave Teri a high five. "Keep digging in that bag," she said, spinning the tearful Maxine around in the salon chair. "There's more."

Almost unable to take any more, Maxine did what they'd asked. Her hands brushed something soft and came out of the bag with a gorgeous chocolate brown mohair sweater. She shrieked, "Oh, my God, oh my God . . ."

"You like it?" Bird asked, her face beaming.

"Like it?" Maxine's gaze tore from sister to sister. "Oh, Bird . . . Teri . . ."

Bird dug in the bag, too impatient for the slow unwrapping process, and handed Maxine a leather-and-tortoiseshell headband that matched the sweater. "No more pulling those pretty shoulder-length locks into Kelly's ponytail scrunchies while you're in class. And put on those small topaz earrings you have, and some slacks—not sweatpants or jeans. Carry a nice handbag, Max—not that huge Mommy pocketbook with diapers and everything but the kitchen sink in it. And wear your little leather flats, no sneakers! Plus, I have the perfect shade of lipstick that will look nice with that new sweater."

All Maxine could do was laugh.

"That's right," Teri fussed as the other stylists began to disperse, leaving good-luck wishes and cheer as they went back to work. "You are a Joseph, and I will not have our family name sullied by my sister going to class all tacky."

"Gotta make a good impression," Bird agreed, flinging a large smock over Maxine, and closing the Velcro fastening at her neck.

"I love you guys," Maxine whispered. "Thank you so much."

"Oh, there's a price," Teri added. "We are all living vicariously through this experience, and we want every single tingle of any details from your class."

"And, we want you to do well," Bird said more seriously. "We want you to thoroughly have a chance to shine. We've got your back."

Maxine just nodded as the room became blurry again. She couldn't believe her sisters were vicariously living through one of *her* experiences, cheering her on and finding real pleasure in her doing well. It put all the spats and fights, growing up and grown, into perspective. Her soul was so filled up with love and joy, she couldn't remember the last time she'd felt this way.

Parking near the community center, Maxine had to will herself to turn off the ignition. This was the moment of truth.

All week she'd been a whirlwind of activity, making sure all her errands were run, chores done, and lunches packed. She'd even left Kenny's dinner on a plate to be microwaved. She didn't start any arguments, and had been so sweet that she was giving herself a cavity. Her sisters had dressed her and bought her new school supplies. She chuckled as she thought of Ahmad and Kelly, the way they had looked at her anxiously and clutched her hand on their first days going to kindergarten. That was just how she felt. What if the teacher was mean? What if he didn't like her? What if the other kids in the school made fun of her because she couldn't write? What if after all the effort to get here, she failed?

Maxine pushed those demons out of her head, turned off the ignition, and got out of the car. She could do this.

Glancing around to be sure that it was safe to walk to the building, she hurried down the street, the wind gusting its full March blast at her back. Once inside the warmth of the center, she walked up to the receptionist's desk. She was early. But that was a good thing; she could pick out a seat near the back of the room and not be so noticed. If she'd gotten there late, all the seats in the back might be filled, and she'd have to sit right up under the teacher—if she remembered how school went.

"Uhmm," she murmured quietly, "I'm signed up for Mr. Paul Gotier's writing class."

"Your name?" the older lady said, glancing down to a registration list.

"Maxine. Maxine Chadway."

The woman before her used her finger to go down the list, and repeated "Chadway" until she found it. "Sign here."

Unziping her new case, Maxine took out a pen that had never been used and signed her name. She stifled the bubbly feeling that made her want to giggle.

"Down the hall to the left, in conference room B."

Maxine nodded and willed herself not to skip as she went. She was in. She was there. She had made it.

But once she got to the door of the conference room, she hesitated. She hadn't been in school in years, and she'd probably be the oldest person in the class. The others who had signed up were probably real authors, or real writers, in any event. She took a deep breath and opened the classroom door, and froze.

There was no back or front of the room. The metal folding chairs had been arranged in a semicircle. And there was nothing on the blackboard. Instead the room hosted a flip chart, and blank sheets of paper had been put up all over the room with masking tape. She glanced at the desk. There was a big coffee mug filled with colored markers, and she sensed that those weren't all for the teacher. Oh, no . . . they were going to have to put stuff on the board, too—which meant that her mistakes and lack of knowledge would be on public display.

Maxine turned around to leave just as the door opened, and she almost bumped into a tall figure that strode through it.

"Oh, my goodness . . . I'm so sorry," she said quickly, realizing that he was holding his now dripping cup of coffee away from his body to avoid being scalded.

A wide, gorgeous, perfect white smile flashed on his face. Maxine looked at her shoes.

"Sir, I'm so sorry. I was early, and was going to, uh, go back out to wait until it was time for class, and didn't see you."

"It's cool, sister. Do come in. We can chat while I get the room ready."

Lord, have mercy. The man's voice had a thick island lilt to it; smooth enough to make her melt where she was standing.

"Oh, let me get that." Maxine stooped to where the coffee had spilled, digging in her inefficient but cute handbag. If she'd followed her first inclination and had brought her real pocketbook, she'd have had Wet Ones in there!

"It's no worry." He smiled, touching her elbow as he dropped a few napkins and mopped up the spill himself. "I was the one carrying my vice through the door without looking where I was headed. I run on coffee

morning and night—a bad habit I continually promise
I'll give up, but the writing at night . . . ahhh, what can
I say? So, you sit, I'll get this up, and then I'll learn
about my early pupil. Okay?"

Maxine just nodded as she watched the man smile
up at her from a squat. Paul Gotier was even finer in
person than he was in his magazine shot. His skin was
the most even, chiseled, dark-walnut-colored marble
she'd ever witnessed in her life! A jet-black mane of
well-coiffed locks fell to his shoulders and framed his
face, which had big, brown, lazy eyes shielded by
unruly, lush, curly black lashes . . . and his body
appeared to be made of granite, if not titanium steel,
underneath his black mock turtleneck sweater. She
forced her gaze away from the muscles that rippled in
his back, shoulders, and arms as he cleaned up the spill,
and she refused to look at the way his thighs bulged out
in his khakis under a squat. A flash of silver at his wrist
from his West Indian bangle made her look at his large,
strong hands. They sure didn't make teachers like this
when she was in school.

She found a seat toward the end of the semicircle, far
away from his desk, and made busywork of removing
her bomber jacket, opening her portfolio, and arranging her purse on the back of her seat. He turned away
to set down his Styrofoam cup of coffee, and she
sneaked a peek. Mr. Gotier looked as good going as
coming. That just wasn't fair. She was a Christian, *married* woman, and temptation was staring her right in
the face.

Paul Gotier turned around and leaned on his desk,
extending his long legs out in front of him and bracing

his weight on his hands. Maxine picked at the rubber holding her pad together. An entire cloud of butterflies had found the pit of her stomach again.

"So," her instructor began in a pleasant tone. "Talk to me. Why have you decided to take this class?"

She just knew this was all a bad idea. She couldn't look at his mouth when he'd spoken; those full, smooth lips were just too much.

"Mr. Gotier—"

"No formalities in my class. This is a creative workshop where we are all peers."

"Peers?" Maxine laughed. "Hardly, sir."

His smile was so brilliant that she almost squinted.

"Every time I teach a class, I learn too. We are all in the process of learning, growing, evolving. Now, my name is Paul. Yours?"

"Maxine. Maxine Chadway."

"Okay, Maxine," he said in his deep, sexy voice. "What do you want to accomplish in these brief six weeks we have together?"

It was hard for her to gather her thoughts. What *did* she really want to accomplish? Paul Gotier waited with such a patient expression that it began to melt her insecurities. He seemed to really want to know what was on her mind, and she sorta liked the way he had put his question. The end of it hung in her mind: "in these brief six weeks we have together," like they, alone, had six weeks to be together.

Maxine shrugged, as much to clear her head of her inappropriate thoughts as to convey that she wasn't sure. "I have all these old journal entries," she replied in an unsure voice. "And I have all these good memories of growing up . . . and I thought maybe I could put them together in some way, so that my children could one day know what it was like growing up in my era."

He laughed, the sound warm and companionable.

"Your era, Maxine? You're making it sound like you're a hundred years old." His eyes twinkled. "That would put me at a hundred and five, then. We'll see what we can do. So talk to me," he repeated.

His accent made the request glide over her and enter her pores. She could almost imagine him saying that to her under different, more erotic circumstances. "Baby, talk to me . . ." Damn, she had to get herself together.

"Uh . . . I'm not sure what you mean."

"You said you have good memories from being a child. What is it that you want your children to remember?"

A smile slowly dawned on her face. "Oh," she murmured, "we had so much fun, even though there were few conveniences."

"Like what?" He'd moved to one of the chart pad sheets hanging on the wall and was wielding a marker. He made everything appear so easy, his motions fluid, relaxed, and unhurried. And he was going to write in front of her—not something of his, but *her* words.

"Well, take games, for example," she said after a moment, glancing down at her pad and then up at him. "We were outside all the time, it seemed. We jumped rope, played hide-and-seek, jacks, kick-the-can, dolls— and made their clothes, no batteries, no video games."

Paul Gotier was scribbling furiously as she spoke, and he gave her an encouraging grunt as he stepped away from the wall. She was sure he was about to say something to her when the conference room door opened and several students came through it.

"Hello!" he boomed, motioning for the other students to take a seat. "Had an early pupil, and we began workshopping. As soon as we have a full room, we'll all introduce ourselves and get started." Then he turned his back to them and addressed Maxine again. "This is good content, and a great place to start. As we develop your concepts in this seminar, we'll work on style, voice, how you want to begin the story, and points of view. Shall we tell it as Maxine the woman in a flashback, or from her perspective as a child? These are techniques that we'll explore. All right?"

She needed to pinch herself again to be sure that she wasn't dreaming. He'd said "we," encouraging her with an excited expression on his face, and appearing, by his body language, to have shut out the other students. Never in a million years would she have expected that.

As the chairs finally filled in around Maxine and her fellow classmates settled in, Paul Gotier took command of the class. Each student was asked to stand up and give a brief history of their writing experiences, and say what they wanted to receive from the class. She watched the instructor's reaction as much as she watched her fellow classmates. He seemed to wince at the people who told him they wanted to write a novel, or who rattled off a series of writing achievements. But why would he do that?

The others had magazine or newspaper articles to their credits, impressive résumés that touted English literature as a college major, and here she was with a raggedy bunch of disjointed journal notes. She was the least skilled, and the only unpublished person in the room. It had felt like a dental exam when it was her turn to stand up and admit that she'd just been writing from time to time as an amateur. Not to mention, she was the oldest student in the class—other than the teacher.

"All right," Gotier said, once the last introduction had been made. "Now, for six weeks, I want you to throw out everything you have learned about writing." He walked over to a blank sheet of paper. "I am interested in assisting you to find your passion on a clean slate. When you find your passion, the voice, the prose, the realism in the work will shine through. The rest is technique, not raw talent. I want you to feel the work, to make it live and breathe when you put it on the page."

The instructor motioned toward a young man who had identified himself as an up-and-coming screenwriter. "Kadim. Tell me what you had to go through to come here tonight."

If anybody would be good at this, Maxine thought, it had to be somebody who wrote screenplays. She was definitely out of her league.

"I waited for my friend," Kadim replied, "and when he didn't show, I took the El over here, and walked a few blocks. That's why I was a little late."

Paul Gotier nodded.

"Okay. How about you, Maxine? You were early— why?"

She wanted to slide into the toes of her shoes and disappear. She *knew* she'd be called on, but just hoped it would be after she got the hang of things. Maxine let her breath out hard and tried to arrange the facts in her head to come up with an intelligent reply.

"Well," she said, releasing a long sigh. "I really wanted to take this class, and I knew I had to get the kids squared away, my husband's dinner ready so he wouldn't make a fuss, and then gather up all my stuff to make sure I had everything. Usually, if I'm rushing, I always have to go back for something, so I checked and double-checked, made sure he could smell dinner—red beans and rice, fried whiting, and some collards—when he came in, and I had a zillion errands to run. I didn't want to walk in here all jangled, and I knew I needed some decompression time because I was nervous. I haven't been in a classroom in I don't know how long."

Maxine took a breath, making eye contact with each student, hoping someone in the room would be able to relate. Then she looked at Paul Gotier, offering him another apology. "So I was too efficient, I guess, got here and realized I was too early, and was about to double back when I almost knocked your coffee out of your hand."

A series of chuckles threaded its way among her fellow students, and Maxine looked down the pen she was clutching. She felt so stupid. Who cared about some housewife's to-do list?

"Perfect!" Paul Gotier threw his head back and laughed.

Perfect? Maxine couldn't believe it.

The classroom went still.

"Did you hear that emotion? Kadim, class, did you hear the difference in those stories?"

Silence met his question.

"People, use your ears." Paul Gotier was walking

around the circle of chairs, forcing students to crane their necks to keep eye contact with him. "I heard exasperation. I smelled food being cooked and left for a spouse, and could almost taste it. I heard nervousness. I heard excitement and determination." He went to the board and began jotting down his points.

"Kadim, how did you feel when your friend didn't show?"

"I was pissed off."

"Okay—what did you do? Did you call him? Did you walk around your home or apartment? What did you do while you were waiting?"

"Oh, yeah . . . I kept playing my CDs, trying not to keep looking down from the window every five minutes."

"And what were you thinking as you walked to the El?"

"How cold it was outside."

"Did you shiver?"

"Hell, yeah."

Laughter echoed through the room.

"Exactly," Paul said, in a satisfied tone. "Maxine opened up your senses. She gave you sight—we can all imagine a bustling household of children, correct? She gave you smell—imagine a home-cooked dinner being made and left to cool on the stove." He wrote each sense down as he continued to speak. "She gave you sound—just by the way she expelled her breath and paused. That is the tone of her story. Now, let's do an exercise that brings in taste and touch. Maxine, please stand. We are going to have an argument. Class—you find each element and chart it. Life is fluid; it moves.

Your writing should transport and move the reader. It must be three-dimensional, not two-dimensional. I want to follow the characters as they move."

"An argument?"

He laughed, grabbing her hand. "Come. Fight with me, Maxine. Start it anywhere you'd like."

On her feet in the middle of the circle, Maxine's free hand found her hip. Desperately trying to ignore the sudden warmth in her palm, she pulled her hand away from his and then folded her arms over her chest.

"I don't know what to argue with you about." She found herself chuckling. This was crazy.

"Yes, you do," he said in a serious tone, walking away from her to lean on the desk.

"I don't, really."

"Why are we going around and around in a circle, then?" He took a sip of his coffee and made a face. "Cold."

"Around in a circle?" Confused, she tilted her head to the side.

"You know what I'm talking about, don't you, Maxine?"

She blinked twice, and just stared at the man. Within seconds, Paul Gotier had pushed himself away from his desk and had rounded it so that the desk was between them. The class was riveted on their exchange, and Maxine felt like she was standing naked in the middle of the floor.

"Why do you insist that you don't know, when you do?"

He'd yelled at her. Actually yelled! Maxine sucked her teeth, and both hands were on her hips in reflex.

"I have never done this before, and I don't know how to do it. I'm sorry!" She walked away from him, totally embarrassed, flopped into her chair, and began doodling on her pad to keep her face from burning with defeat.

Applause greeted her, and she glanced up.

"Perfection!" her instructor boomed. "Electric. Talk to me, people," he implored, going from student to student. "Myra, what happened out there in the circle?"

The young woman with orange-toned braids smiled shyly. "She was confused, and her tone began as open, amused, conciliatory. . . . But the more you pressed, the more frustrated she became. First she was willing to follow your lead to the front of the room when you held her hand, but she drew it back."

"The touch," Paul exclaimed, nodding.

"You tasted the coffee, and it was either cold or you were speaking about her actions as a double entendre when you made a face," another student yelled out.

"Precisely. Then what happened to Maxine's body language?"

"It closed off," another student said quickly. "She got angry because she couldn't fathom what you were talking about or accusing her about. Then she walked away from you, flopped down, and ignored you."

"Probably hoping I'd go away," Paul Gotier laughed. "Very good." His eyes sparkled with mischief as he gazed at Maxine with a supportive smile. "When you all turn in your weekly assignments, I want to feel passion in them. I want to know where the people are in the room, what they are doing or fidgeting with, and why. I want to know if it is hot or cold in there. I want to know what they sound like on the exterior, and also what's cooking in their brains. I want to see their body language come to life on the page, and hear not just dialogue, but the breaths, the pauses, the nonverbal suck of their teeth." He laughed and turned his attention to the other students.

"Make me see it, feel it, taste it, smell it, hear it." Paul Gotier walked as he ticked off his instructions. "Even silence has a sound. It can be sad. It can be angry. It can scream at you and be deafening. What is the white noise in the background of your piece—the hum of a fan, traffic, CDs, as Kadim said? Children? The neighbors next door, or their TV? Talk to me, people."

Maxine was scribbling notes like the others, as fast as she could without taking her eyes off her teacher—a genius, in her estimation. He was explaining things so vividly, and she could understand what he was saying. She didn't feel dumb, or at a disadvantage.

He was telling them to be observant of their environment and to catalog every detail and aspect of what they experienced. This was exactly what she'd wanted to do—to create a memory that went beyond the yellowing Kodak snapshots she had stuffed into photo albums. She wanted her children to taste her mama's cooking. Wanted them to smell Lemon Pledge coming off the furniture. Wanted them to feel the plastic slipcovers on the sofa stick to their butts in the summertime. She needed them to hear all those old-timey sayings that her parents had said to her, and to know what they really meant, depending on the tone that was used when they were said. She wanted them to *feel* what it was like growing up in her world . . . and to have something that lived for them long after she was gone.

"That's what I want to do," she murmured to herself.

"Pardon, Maxine?" Paul Gotier had stopped mid-sentence, and had walked toward her.

Again, she froze. She was talking to herself, not the class, and now she was busted.

"I was just thinking out loud," she said with a self-conscious chuckle.

"Share it," he said. It was a command, but one that played around the corners of his mouth with a relaxed smile. "Please. You have so much life experience that would be helpful to the group."

Flattered beyond measure, Maxine smiled and felt the tension at being caught slip away. "I have all these old photos of my family," she said in a quiet voice. "Especially of my parents, who are gone now. And there are such rich memories that the camera just can't convey. Like the way my mama talked to her pots as she was cooking, or the way my daddy whistled when he was working out in the garage . . . so many sights, sounds, tastes, smells, and feels that I want to leave behind for my kids. When my parents passed on, all I had left were inanimate objects . . . nothing that made me hear their voices again. I was thinking about that as I was taking notes, and I said, 'That's what I want to do.' Crazy, huh?"

Her teacher's expression softened, and he took an empty chair away from the circle, turned it around, and sat down right in front of Maxine. His eyes seemed like they would drink her in.

"Class, I want you to take notes on what this remarkable woman just said. She is here to follow her passion. Her mission is to leave a living family legacy. It doesn't matter whether or not it has commercial value—that's not her goal. She wants to make the important characters from her existence live eternally on the pages of her work—not to get paid, not to win an award, not to satisfy her own ego, but for the simplicity of the gift of telling the story . . . passing the torch. I am honored to have such a student? Ms. Chadway. Thank you for gracing my class."

Just as abruptly as he'd sat, he stood, put the chair back, and was walking again. Maxine sat stunned. *He* was honored to have *her* in *his* class?

"This," he said sweeping his arm toward Maxine, "is a novelist." You could have heard a pin drop in the room. "Why?" Paul Gotier allowed his gaze to land on each face. "Because she is intimate with the details of her surroundings, she will pay attention to every voice inflection, action, and reaction—because she is writing about something she is passionate about. And, ladies and gentlemen, this is not something they can teach you in school—you have to feel it."

Maxine had to remember to breathe.

"Next week," he instructed, "I want each of you to bring in the first passage or chapter of what you have written on your most current project. Make a copy of the first five pages for use in class. We are going to break up into small groups of two or three people, and see if the writing lives on the page, or if it is dead and two-dimensional. Next week, people, we are going to get real. And," he said with a serious expression in his eyes, "adjectives do not make me feel it. Do not come in here with long, expository musings that have fifty adjectives per paragraph, because I will hurt your feelings. Be forewarned."

Then just like that, he shook his wrist to make the thick silver bangle around it slide up his forearm so that he could peer at his watch. He nodded, clapped his hands, and dismissed the class on two words. "Next week."

"Hey, Kenny."

"Hi."

From his stakeout position on the sofa, Kenny watched his wife float in the door. He had to admit that she looked radiant. As she took off her jacket, he noticed that she'd literally transformed herself for this class. She had her hair down on her shoulders and held back off her face with some new little headband he hadn't seen before. Her hair was glossy, and no doubt Bird had a hand in that. Maxine even had on a touch of makeup. Her lashes were thick, there was a glow to her cheeks, and she was wearing lipstick—like she was going to church or something.

And where did she get that new brown sweater? Not to mention, why did she have on her good slacks, instead of jeans? She had the nerve to sashay into the house all smiles, like she'd been out clubbing or something, and that leather briefcase-looking thing had to cost a mint.

"How was class?" he muttered as she came toward him.

"Fan*tas*tic," she replied, brushing his forehead with a kiss, and then going straight for the kitchen.

She had brushed his head with a kiss. His *forehead,*

not his mouth, like he was one of the children! He watched her retreat toward the kitchen with her new portfolio, surveying how nice her butt looked in the light wool pants she wore. As he considered how to go into the kitchen behind her, without it seeming obvious that he wanted more than a one-word answer about her first night at class, he heard Maxine's laughter. Her sisters had beat him to the punch.

More correctly, Maxine had beaten him to the punch. She hadn't even waited for him to inquire further. She just made a beeline to the telephone and dialed either Teri or Bird or both. Why couldn't she have sat on the sofa with him and given him the headlines? Why wasn't he the first in on the scoop? How come all he got from her was grief, or one-liners, and her sisters apparently got the full, ripened story?

Her squeals and hushed tones, interspersed with hearty laughter, made him stand and walk toward the stairs. He had other people he could talk to, or share his day with, besides her—like Lem . . . not that Lem had been any help this week, ribbing him about not wanting to be in the doghouse like him. But he had friends, too, since she was making it clear that he was no longer her friend. Fine. He had to get up early in the morning to go to work, anyway.

seven

nothing was going to stand in Maxine's way. She was totally focused. Her sisters were behind her, and there was nothing for her husband to argue about, even though he had remained salty about practically everything all week, even through Sunday dinner with the whole family. But she didn't even worry about that, because she had a hundred pages of her memories cataloged and ready for class. She wasn't even worried about coming into the center twenty minutes early this time. If the kids would just get out from underfoot so she could go!

"Mom, can I talk to you for a second?"

Ahmad stood in the kitchen doorway. Impatience seized her, but Maxine let her breath out slowly and responded as calmly as possible. "Sure, but I can't be late to class tonight. Aunt Teri is coming by in a few—"

"You ever think that maybe Dad is worried, and maybe that's why he's so against everything?"

Maxine let pass the fact that her son had cut her off, and studied the young face before her. "Oh, Ahmad, your father doesn't have a thing to worry about. Now, are we talking about him, or you?" She smiled and held her son's serious gaze.

"Maybe we both are," he said in a quiet voice.

The tone of her son's comment made Maxine's smile disappear. "Why would my writing bother either of you?"

"It's not the writing, Mom," Ahmad said in a near whisper. "You know Dad has never been good at helping any of us with homework and stuff, even though he tries. And maybe . . . well, maybe he's worried because all of a sudden you have your own friends, and look all pretty—like you're going somewhere—and he only has the business? Maybe because you're good at a lot of academic things, and he's not . . . well . . ."

She went to the teenager who was trying his best to wrap his mind around something as complex as a marriage, enfolded her son in her arms for a moment, then let him go. "Your Dad and I have been through a lot of ups and downs, but we love each other," she assured him. "And like I told you before, there are some things between married people that nobody else can figure out—so let me work on your father. Deal?"

He nodded, but she could tell her boy wasn't convinced. She studied the wisdom in his face and thought of her mother. There was so much of Mama Joe in him.

"Just promise that you'll include Dad in the stuff you write about. Maybe that'll make him feel better . . . to know you were thinking about him, too."

Maxine's smile returned as she brushed her son's forehead with a kiss. "I think about your dad more than you know," she replied. But how much did Kenny think of her these days? "I couldn't write about this family without him."

Seeming mollified, her son stepped aside to let her pass. As she made the rounds, kissing each child good-bye and giving them explicit instructions to behave for their aunt, she wondered how many other students had to get full sanctions just to go to school. Part of her was grateful for the gift of being cared for this way, yet another part of her felt resentful. Kenny walked in and out of the door at will; she couldn't. She was Mom.

When Maxine opened the conference room door, Paul Gotier looked up from his desk and beamed at her. The warm greeting sent a shiver of anticipation through her.

"My early bird is here," he announced, unfurling his tall, athletic body from the chair.

"I was so psyched from last week's class, I couldn't wait to get here," Maxine admitted.

"Well? Let me see what you've got."

She pulled off her jacket, plopping her pocketbook on the chair that she claimed, and quickly walked to his desk with her portfolio like an expectant schoolgirl.

"I did a hundred pages. Twenty pages a day, almost."

"Wow," he murmured, accepting the stack of paper from her hands and studying the pages. "I'm impressed."

"I've had so much on my mind, so many things just bottled up that I wanted to say and get out, that I even surprised myself."

Her teacher nodded, his gaze riveted on the work in his hands. "I can tell you did this all in one big computer file, instead of breaking it up into chapters." He looked up.

Her heart sank at his criticism. "Yeah—"

"I'm only telling you this because I wouldn't want

you to lose any of this wonderful work. When you go back into your computer, make each chapter its own file—it's also easier to edit it that way."

His comments had been guidance, she realized, not a slam against what she'd created. Maxine quickly bobbed her head in agreement. "I can do that. I'll get on it as soon as I get home. I hadn't thought of that."

"Just a safety trick I had to learn the hard way, Maxine." He chuckled in an easy manner and shook his head. "I don't want to hear your scream in the dead of night—a writer's worst nightmare is having your hard drive crash, all your work gone, and then you're on your knees trying to barter with God. Ask me one day how I know."

They shared companionable laughter, and then Paul Gotier picked up his pen. A red ink pen. Maxine almost closed her eyes at the scalpel he was surely going to wield on her beloved creation. He gave her a calm, reassuring smile when she cringed.

"I've done this before. The patient can be saved, but needs a little cosmetic surgery." Then he winked at her. "You can look away while I cut, if you need to."

He had a way of disarming her and relaxing her at the same time. It made her blush, so she kept her eyes focused on the papers on his desk as he edited. Broad strokes of red spilled out across the cuts he made, and she felt like she was watching blood run.

But Paul Gotier spoke smoothly, his voice even and his tone reassuring as he dissected her work.

"Just at first glance," he told her, making her look at his markings, "you have groups of thought. These need to be chapters, or grouped some other way. For exam-

ple, you have Sunday dinners, going to church, cama-
raderie in the kitchen, sibling fights." All of a sudden,
he threw his head back and laughed.

Maxine wasn't quite sure how to read that, so she
just held her breath and waited. His eyes twinkled as his
gaze remained on a page. He shook his head and
laughed low in his throat, and then looked up at her.

"Oh, Max. This is so rich, so wonderful. All you
have to do is organize it, and get it in the right format."

She thought she might simply float away. "You think
so?"

"I know so," he replied, holding her gaze for a
moment and then looking back down at the pages.
"You need to get this in manuscript format, however."
He glanced up at her again. "Double-spaced, one-inch
margins, with a header on every page—delineated by
chapter, pages numbered. Right now you have it single-
spaced."

"Oh, I can fix that," she said quickly, wishing that
she'd known some of this before she started.

"That will make it easier for you to see your own
mistakes, too—and for an editor to do what I'm doing
now. That's an industry standard."

"Right, Paul. I'll fix that."

He held up his hand. "Don't panic. It's a common
beginner's error. But if you are going to submit this to
publishing houses, I see no reason to have it discarded
out of hand just for a formatting error." Again he
glanced up. "Have your children ever entered essay con-
tests?"

The question caught Maxine off guard. "Yes."

"Well, it's the same thing. Think of it that way. The

judges won't even read your entry if it's too long, or if the format isn't like they instructed for the contest. You understand now?"

She nodded. It made so much sense.

"They get in a lot of work, and they won't even bother to read it if it isn't according to the standards." He fished in his pocket, pulled out his business card, and handed it to her. "Look on my website. There are links to a lot of research locations that go into details about format, style, grammar, tips that can be helpful, and other things that we don't need to spend class time on."

Again she nodded, holding the card as though he'd dropped a diamond in her palm. As other students began to filter into the classroom, she knew her brief private audience with the writing Zen master was over.

"Thanks so much," she murmured, backing away from the desk.

"You have a duplicate copy of the first five pages, correct?"

"Yeah, just like you told us to. I just brought in all of what I had. . . . I don't know why, but—"

"May I keep these hundred or so pages to really look over?"

Was he kidding? He could keep them forever, and she'd bronze-cast his scribbling on her marked-up pages.

"Sure." Again, she had to remember to breathe.

"Next week, after class, we'll sit and have some coffee, and I'll critique what I've read. But meanwhile, you bang off more of this work—in separate files." He smiled, and then stood to greet the others in the class.

* * *

The rest of the evening had been surreal. From the moment he'd asked to keep her work, she could hardly concentrate. But she'd participated with gusto in her group, and had taken so many notes that her hand was cramping as she held the steering wheel to drive home. Teri and Bird would be so proud, they'd flip! Paul Gotier had asked *her* out to coffee, alone, for a private critique session.

"Teri!" she practically screamed into the cell phone. "Get Bird on the line, too."

"Where are you, Maxine?"

"In the car. This couldn't wait until I got home. I gave him my pages!"

"What? Hold on. Let me get Bird."

Maxine drummed her fingers on the steering wheel as she waited impatiently for Bird to click on. As soon as she heard her other sister's voice join her and Teri on the line, she launched into a full recount of the class.

"Now you know Kenny is going to have a cow," Bird laughed.

"What Kenny doesn't know won't hurt him," Maxine heard herself say. But her laughing comment was met by silence.

"I don't know if that's a good idea," Teri suggested. "He *is* your husband."

Again, silence. Maxine watched the traffic light turn from red to green as a strange defensiveness rose within her. She'd thought they were on her side.

"Y'all know how Kenny has been about my taking this class," she pressed, hoping to regain their allegiance. "He doesn't want to hear about my writing or

share in any good news about it, and I've kept everything going smoothly at home—haven't given him a
thing to complain about. Dinner is fixed for him, even
though the kids eat with you all. The house is tidy,
lunches made, nothing has changed. So why can't I
have a cup of coffee with my teacher—who is going to
give my work a thorough critique?"

Her sisters were slow to respond, and it nagged her.

"I think is it really wonderful that your work is good
enough to have captured your instructor's attention like
it has," Teri said, her tone controlled and cautious.
"That's not the part I have a problem with."

"Then what is it?" Maxine snapped, feeling attacked
and not sure why.

"The problem is," Bird interjected, "that if you are
going to go out with your professor for a cup of coffee,
and it's strictly legitimate business, then you need to tell
Kenny where you are going and who you are going
with, so there'll be no misunderstandings—since it is a
male teacher."

Maxine sighed. She hated the logic that was blowing
her high. "All right, all right. But you know how
Kenny is. I just didn't want to deal with his negative
attitude, or start an argument about something so
silly."

"I hear you," Bird conceded.

Although Maxine relaxed a bit, still, Bird's comment
annoyed her. Teri's silence now sounded like an accusation. And what did her sister mean by, "If it's legitimate
business"? Of course it was legitimate business. What,
now she had to explain her every action to even them?
It was hard enough to direct her good news and devel-

opments only to her sisters and shield it from Kenny's negative input; the thought of not being able to fully share with them made her sad.

Suddenly weary, she no longer wanted to tell them every single detail of tonight. She didn't want to go into how her stomach felt when the man cast an approving glance in her direction, or put his hand on her shoulder, peering down at her group's developments. She didn't want to describe how good he looked in his jeans and turtleneck sweater, or discuss his cologne, or his million-dollar smile against that dark, beautiful skin of his. Nor did she want to explain how validated she felt by his earnest compliments of her work.

"Maxine," Teri said after a moment. "Listen, honey, we're all still rooting for you. There's no harm in having a professional mentor. It's just that—"

"We don't want to see you make more of it than it is," Bird chimed in, "and possibly get yourself into trouble."

Now her sisters were getting on her nerves. Maxine almost ran a red light and had to slam on the brakes.

"I just *respect* the man. That's all," Maxine argued. "He's brilliant—and for the first time in my life, I have somebody to *really* take an interest in something I'm doing. He respects me—critiques my work, and gives me guidance, and is gentle with the criticism, and—"

"And is everything Kenny hasn't been, lately," Teri interrupted in a flat tone.

"And is fine, sexy, accomplished, and single," Bird added with a sigh.

"And makes your stomach do flip-flops," Teri added with emphasis.

"And is treating you like you wish your husband would," Bird reminded her.

"And obviously thinks you are something special—which is something you haven't felt in a while, as you've told us. We aren't making this up," Teri said, her voice logical and mellow.

"Which is why we are saying, Stay grounded, be careful, and tell your husband where you are going," Bird insisted. "Maxine, when your husband is getting on your nerves, the grass *always* looks greener on the other side. I know that well."

Maxine opened her mouth to make a rebuttal, but then closed it. There was a lot of truth in what her sisters had said. There were things going on inside her that she didn't even want to admit to herself: like the fact that ever since she'd been in Paul Gotier's class, her husband had become less and less physically appealing to her. She'd been able to sleep right through Wednesday nights and Saturday nights without even missing them.

"All right," Maxine finally conceded. "I'll tell him where I'm going, but I'm not asking for permission from him anymore—about anything. I'm grown."

When Bird chuckled, she felt better.

"I've been telling you that all along, Maxine," her sister chided.

"We didn't say ask Kenny," Teri said. "We said be up-front and *inform* him. You don't have to ask him about furthering your career goals—just stay on the up and up."

"That's right," Bird added. "Don't do like men do, and start sliding and slipping here and there. Be honest, and then you don't have a thing to apologize for, explain, or hide."

"Yeah. That's right," Maxine said with more confidence. "I don't know what I was thinking. I just didn't feel like getting a bunch of static."

"We hear you," her sisters said in unison, laughing as they spoke.

She'd expected Kenny to be waiting up again and sitting on the sofa, looking annoyed and pretending to read a newspaper, but he wasn't. Good. Nothing else to blow her classroom high.

Maxine sauntered over to the stereo and clicked it on—something she rarely did alone. She let the soft music waft over her as she stretched out on the couch, needing some time to think about everything that had happened and had been said. Her son's nagging doubts fused with her sisters', and she pushed the negative thoughts away. What was wrong with a person utilizing a gift that had never fully developed? Plus, she'd learned so much in class tonight, and the other students were giving her as much respect as they did those with some published work. But the best part of all was Paul Gotier's attention.

Closing her eyes, she replayed every moment of their exchanges. He was the kindest but toughest, most encouraging teacher she'd ever known. He could just take an awkward sentence and flip it, and then re-create it into something that worked without destroying the originator's voice. And although he beat up the class tonight, it was with that old-fashioned brand of firmness—the way those old black teachers in school would demand excellence because they believed in their students and wouldn't accept less. Made you work to be twice as good, even if you only got half the credit.

Just thinking about the man and his style and his command of a classroom made her want to go to her laptop, but she reveled a while longer in her thoughts. Her mind began to wander. She wondered if Paul Gotier was as kind and firm and patient with his children as he was with his students in class. And the man obviously had religion; he'd made a reference to being on one's knees praying to God if the computer crashed. Yeah . . . he was a good man all around. His wife had to be a lunatic to let that go.

His voice alone would have kept me there, she thought, chuckling to herself. Before she knew it, her mind had wrapped itself around his smooth island lilt and was substituting one of his classroom phrases into an imaginary romantic encounter. "Talk to me, baby," her brain replayed in Paul Gotier's rich accent, along with his intense way of staring at his students. Once the voice-activated fantasy took root, she began to imagine that fine specimen of maleness without his sweater and jeans on. Locked in her own thoughts, she felt her body heat and stir in a way it hadn't in a long while.

Common sense was trying to wrestle with the image and make it go away, but a sensual section of her brain was on automatic. It had been so long since she'd made love, or wanted to—weeks. She could just imagine his patient style in bed . . . with those steady hands, delicious-looking mouth, and that body. Maxine sat up fast. This was *not* a good thing.

The only man she'd ever been with was Kenny. True,

she'd admired other fine men before, but had never gone this far. Her son's words and worry cloaked her. Had Ahmad picked up something that she'd unwittingly transmitted? Had her sisters? Had Kenny! What was she thinking of?

She stood up and went into the kitchen. She couldn't go to sleep now. What if she started feeling like this in their bed?

Maxine went to the refrigerator and found the iced tea. She'd just type a little and cool herself down, then go back to the routine of her home. That's all she had to do. Push it out of her head. Then she froze, setting down the pitcher. Had she given any inappropriate signals to her teacher? Oh, Lord . . . She prayed she hadn't. Maybe that's why Bird and Teri were on her case—maybe her sisters had picked something up. Her mind ran through everything that she'd said and done in the last couple of weeks. Drawing a blank, she slowly began to relax. No. Bird and Teri were just anticipating disaster, but no disaster had occurred. Or would occur. And Ahmad was just feeling the silent strain between her and Kenny, that was all.

She walked over to the cabinets and took down a glass, dismayed at her feelings. She had to stop acting like a foolish schoolgirl with a crush. That's all it was. A crush. And her sisters had picked it up, simply because they knew her. No, more like they knew her circumstances.

Maxine poured her iced tea and took a swig of it with frustration. Yeah, they knew how Kenny never took her out, or listened to her these days. They knew that the closest thing her husband could come up with for a romantic gesture was some half-hearted attempt at flipping on the stereo, cutting off the lights, and buying a cheap bottle of wine. And then, he didn't have anything to talk about to her. And she wondered why she was fixated on some sexy, nice, considerate, intelligent, capable, religious, supportive man?

"Pullease," Maxine murmured in a huff as she returned the pitcher of sweet tea to the refrigerator.

She sat down at the kitchen table with the intention of editing her passages, but found her gaze drawn to the window. Didn't men fantasize from time to time? Didn't they go to strip bars and imagine, even if they didn't touch? She hadn't done *that*, so what was the big deal? She should allow herself the freedom of privately thinking about some fantasy without guilt chasing the wonderful image away. Kenny had her conditioned . . . or maybe she had her own damned self conditioned. Whatever. Paul Gotier was a nice image to have in one's mind.

Sipping her tea slowly, she wondered about all of it. What if she'd met someone like him before she'd met Kenny? What if she hadn't married her high school sweetheart, and then bumped into that hunk? What if she were free to go down to St. Lucia with a man like that? She had to close her eyes at the very thought of it. Deep sexy voice in her ear, strong dark hands stroking all the want up and out of her body through her pores. "Mmmm." In a villa set on a white sand beach, lush trees bearing fruit all around, turquoise blue water so clear you could see the sand crabs walking by your feet . . .

A shaft of heat pierced her and made her open her

eyes. She didn't know whether to laugh or cry. All she did know was, her husband had better get himself together and treat her like she was worth something. Kenny needed to take some interest in her, before somebody else did—because she liked how that felt. He'd better come with a little conversation and a little courting, like he used to, if he wanted her to be in the mood. He'd had it his way for too long.

Kenny had just better make an effort to start understanding his wife.

When Kenny woke up, he searched Maxine's side of the bed. It was cold. She hadn't even bothered to come to bed last night. Renewed frustration lit within him, and he immediately went on a search for his wife.

He'd briefly panicked until he heard the stereo on the jazz station. That had to be Maxine's doing. None of the kids would have turned to that station. But it was six-thirty A.M. So what if he had gone to bed pissed off and hadn't waited up for her? That was no cause for her not to come to bed. He'd heard her come in at the normal time, but he wasn't going to sit there and be ignored again while she chatted away on the telephone with her sisters.

His anger gaining momentum, Kenny paced through the living room and into the kitchen—where he stopped in the doorway and stared. Maxine had fallen asleep on the kitchen table. Her head was down on her arms, the computer was still on, and she had a stack of papers next to her. She'd even left half a glass of iced tea beside the empty pitcher. See, this was just what he'd been trying to tell her. She needed to focus on the household, instead of these writing escapades.

"Maxine," he boomed, loud enough to rouse her. "Do you know what time it is?"

She slowly lifted her head, looked around with sleepy eyes, and yawned. "Oh, wow . . . I must have dozed off while repairing these chapters."

"Yeah, well, the kids are still asleep, and the kitchen is a mess, and—"

She held up one hand to cut him off. "I know. I got caught up in what I was doing. I'll rush them, so they won't be late. Relax."

"Relax?"

"Yeah, Kenny, for once in your life, get off my back. I'm tired."

Shocked, he just stood there and gaped at her. She didn't even pretend to care what he thought. Nor did she seem very concerned that she might have made the children late for school. In fact, her reply sounded like something a guy would say to his wife, not the other way around. *He* was the one standing in the doorway speaking to the errant spouse who had come in after hanging out. He did not like this role, and he wasn't dealing with this twisted script.

"Now see here, Maxine—"

"Kenny," she snapped, standing and gathering her papers while shutting down the computer, "I've had enough of your nonsense. Look around this house. Is there anything, save an iced tea glass and an empty pitcher, that is out of order?"

"Well, no, but—"

"Have I been somewhere I'm not supposed to be?"

"Well, no, but—"

"Did I go out drinking and come in drunk, or did I come home and do something productive?"

This was not how the conversation was supposed to go.

"Yeah, but—"

"Then back off." Maxine snapped the laptop closed and glared at him. "When's the last time you took a real interest in anything I was doing, huh?"

"That's not true." He had to say something to defend himself.

"You don't even know my favorite color, let alone what I'm working on here. You've only read my work when a gun was practically put to your head; you only ask me to go out in a harsh voice, like an order. You want everything to go your way, when you want it, like you want it, and damn what I want."

She had paced to the stove and turned on the water for the tea. Not the coffeemaker, he noted.

"When's the last time you brought me some flowers, just because? If you saw that I was dog tired enough to fall asleep on the kitchen table, why didn't you wake the children get them started, and perhaps inconvenience yourself a little bit, for once? It never occurred to you to make the kids' lunch for the next day since I was going to school at night, did it? No, because your self-righteous ass thinks that I shouldn't be trying to improve myself, and your goal is to make me feel every moment of my errant ways, right? But I already knew that about you. So I make the lunches before I leave, just like I cook you dinner—although there's *never* a plate of the food I cooked waiting for me."

She shook her head, not even looking in his direction. "Would've been nice if you woke up, just because you didn't feel my body heat next to you, and came down to put a blanket over my shoulders—or to say, 'Baby, come to bed.' Instead, you come down here all puffed up and righteous."

"I wanted you to come to bed," he murmured, her accusations dulling his rage and allowing guilt to settle in its place. "But I figured you didn't want to."

"Truth be told, I didn't." She held his shocked gaze locked within her own. "Why would I? Do you talk to me sweet in my ear? Do you encourage me, or support me, or do anything outside of bed that makes me want to fall into your arms like I used to? Do you take your time and love me nice and slow, like you used to? Or do you just roll over, hit it, and quit it? Do you even know what turns me on anymore? Do you even recognize that half of the process of turning a woman on has to do with what happens *outside* the bedroom—and not just gymnastics within it? No. So why on earth, would I want to come to our bed?"

Her words both stunned and frightened him. They contained too much stark truth for a morning discussion. Her voice had not even risen; it was calm, factual, and with a tone of contempt. Maxine had never sounded like that before—not to him. His brain needed time to align the facts, to develop a response.

"Next week, I'll be late," she announced, her hands on her hips. "My work is being individually critiqued—because it's *that good*, Kenny. Not that you would know, since you only read a few poems under duress. But that is a part of the class. So, again, you don't have to wait up."

She had made a statement, and there was no question in her tone.

He nodded. "Okay." Then he walked away to go wake up the children.

He didn't like this new wife of his. She scared him. She had turned into a person he didn't know. He missed the old Maxine but somehow knew that person was gone forever. This wasn't like the other times, when she was doing something new on a temporary basis, and time would bring her back—like it had when he'd recovered from the car accident and she could leave Chadway Towing and come home again. Nor was it like that political race: even a campaign had an end to it. But there would be no end to the writing, even if the class would be over in six weeks.

And who was this Paul Gotier person, who instilled so much confidence in Maxine about her work? He should have looked at the magazine Bird mentioned.

Curiosity haunted him as he drove home from work. Curiosity became a siren as he pulled over in front of a newsstand. Curiosity knew no shame as he picked up an *Essence* magazine and flipped through it, ignoring the weird stares of the men in line. Curiosity was a bitch, when he saw who had his wife for six weeks. No wonder Maxine had lost her mind.

Kenny paid for the magazine without a word. He needed to read this article, really study the photo. People always looked better in a picture than in real life—the way they could take out imperfections with special effects cameras and whatnot. Yeah, he'd read all about the guy, and then he'd have *a lot* to talk to Maxine about when she came home.

Three weeks of not sleeping together. Why, because he was supposed to now turn into a scholar? Kenny pulled away from the curb, burning rubber.

"Look," Paul Gotier instructed, sliding a page of Maxine's story across the diner table toward her and reading it upside down. "There are redundant passages that will make your story drag." He began drawing big red blocks around sections of her prose as he quickly flipped the pages. "See, like here, and here. You have already described what a summer is like in Chicago from a child's perspective. Wonderful descriptions. You've given me, here, see here, winter, and then in this section, what it's like as the seasons transition to get ready for school, or over here, to anticipate spring."

He looked up at her and smiled. "Don't be alarmed. I'm not blocking these passages to cut them, but to allow you to decide which portions to keep or shed. This is the part that not even an editor can do for you. But you don't have to describe the same things over and over."

She nodded, and he covered her hand with his own.

"Maxine, there were parts of this story where I laughed until I wiped my eyes. There were other parts that choked me up so badly I had to put the work down, do some chore around the house, and then pick it back up again. You have a voice that rings so true, it made me remember growing up myself."

He held her gaze for a moment, and then removed his hand from hers as though she'd burned him. He took a quick swig of his coffee before speaking—all the while keeping his focus on the papers before him.

"The redundant descriptions frustrate the reader. Once you've described a scene or a room, you don't have to describe it again—like each time a character walks through the Joseph living room. We already know what it looks like, how the plastic feels in each season. Things like that. Make sense?"

He glanced up with a slow smile, and she nodded. Her heart slammed against the inside of her chest from the emotions struggling within it. There was deep admiration colliding with appreciation, awe, a touch of raw lust peeking out behind what felt like friendship, and trust.

"Paul, thank you so much."

She stared at this man who was her teacher, mentor, possibly a friend, and she could have sworn that his lids lowered a little, those thick, curly lashes covering his eyes. It had happened when she'd said his name, which of its own volition had come out of her mouth on a low syllable that had been stuck within her chest. Maybe she was just imagining things, but she'd lived with a man long enough to know that she wasn't.

"This work is so rich with visual images," he practically breathed. "Maxine . . . where have you been hiding all this time?"

His question was thick with a tone she didn't want to name, and his compliment had rushed out with such passion, it almost scared her. Almost.

"Paul, this is just stuff from my diary and old journals I used to keep." She gave a nervous chuckle, then took a sip of coffee. She had to when he'd briefly shut his eyes, when she'd said his name again. It was odd, but she felt deliciously wanton and very sensual, sitting there flirting a tad. She wasn't going too far, just flirting a little.

She could feel him fight to tear his gaze away from hers and force himself to look down at the pages again. And that felt *so* good. It had been a really long time since a man had to actually make himself look at something else to keep from looking at her. Maxine sipped her hot coffee slowly, and watched Paul. It wasn't only that he was handsome; he was nice, too, which made him all the more attractive.

"Okay," he said, his voice more businesslike. "Here's another thing I want you to work on." He glanced up and used his finger as a pointer across the page. "You see, here? Wonderful, explosive narrative. Then, you've diluted the impact of the emotions in that passage by burying this great phrase in a garble of description." He drew a line through it, and wrote it by hand on a line alone below. "Let it stand by itself. Now read it," he ordered, turning the page around for her to do so. "See how it sounds stronger, crisper?"

"Wow. That's brilliant—it makes all the difference in the world."

He nodded, seeming very pleased, and slightly flushed by her compliment.

"Do it with dialogue, too, Maxine. Don't keep telling me what your mother's favorite sayings were. Make her speak for herself. Let the one-liners come out of her mouth in stand-alone dialogue. Your readers will laugh, identify, and start talking out loud to themselves while they read."

"You make this look so easy, Paul. My goodness. This would have been such a mess without your guidance."

"No," he deferred, shaking his head. "All you see is the result of years of having editors kick my behind. It's not brilliance, just the school of hard knocks." He chuckled. "I'm telling you nicely, because I would hate to have a beautiful woman like you get eaten alive in New York. They're tough up there in the publishing towers. We might be able to avoid some of that."

"This is *not* even *hardly* going to New York," she said, laughing.

He stared at her. "What do you mean, it's not going to New York?"

She didn't know what to say to him. "Uh, this is just for my cedar chest, and my sisters and kids. It's not good enough to—"

"Maxine, who has been tap dancing on your self-esteem?" Paul sat back in his chair and folded his arms over his chest. "It can't be the Joseph family I read about in this wonderful story. So, who made you think you couldn't send a respectable manuscript to New York and have it published?"

"Uh, I . . . I don't know."

"Sure, like all of us, you'll get rejected by dozens of publishers—which doesn't mean this thing can't go to print, or that it's not worthy of print. Rejections come for a lot of reasons and mean a lot of things. Timing, the market, the budgets, whatever. But as one writer to another, I'm telling you, this is good work."

He unfolded his arms then clasped her hand within both of his. "Maxine, Maxine, Maxine," he whispered. "If you don't finish this, if you hide this, and don't try, you will break my heart. I can't even watch it happen."

He let her hand go and sighed, and then cast his gaze

out of the window. She was as stunned, flushed, and tingly as though he'd kissed her. And not a peck-on-the-cheek type kiss, but a whip-a-sister-around, dip-low, bend-her-back, and let-her-have-it type kiss. She was breathless and needed to steady herself before she said a word. He'd kissed her soul.

"Do you have an agent?" he asked, still looking out the window.

"What?" she squeaked.

"An agent. Someone to help move this novel, once it's complete."

She stared at his profile. She couldn't speak.

"It has almost everything in there. Old beliefs, customs, a feel for the times, the transition to a new era. The old giving way to the new. Coming of age. But there are three things it doesn't have: the honesty in the childhood sections isn't there in the coming-of-age passages, and the book doesn't have a hook, or an ending."

Now he was staring at her. But all she could do was keep her eyes on the light tan brew in her cup.

"I'm not sure what you mean," she whispered.

He chuckled. "Yes, you do, and we're going to have that same fight that we had the first day of class." When she glanced up, he chuckled more deeply. "Remember that, 'Yes, you do, no, I don't' mock argument demonstration?"

She offered a slow smile at the memory.

"I'm going to explain to you why you held back in the later part of the book," he said.

"I didn't hold back."

"Hmmm," he murmured. "Everything up to that point was safe, and you could easily tell any of that to your children. Then you hit the adolescent years, and the prose went so flat I knew you were struggling to self-edit."

She blinked twice, gaped, and then put her hand over her heart and laughed.

"Am I on target?"

Her hands went to her face as she nodded and laughed harder.

"You don't have to be explicit," he soothed while laughing with her. "You don't have to get into where people's knees or elbows fit, but you need to be honest, Maxine. Especially when you've treated your readers to honesty all the way through."

Now this was a friend, a real in-your-face, tell-the-truth conversation . . . one that didn't judge but allowed room for self-revelation within laughter. She peeked out from behind her fingers and then dropped her hands. "Oh, Paul. I got stuck. I was so embarrassed. I just didn't know what to say at that point."

"And, it showed, dear lady. What is 'cute,' when describing that first, mind-blowing kiss? Huh? You even lost your handle on the vernacular from that era, you were so flustered. The boy would have been described as 'sharp' in his robin's-egg blue suit, right?"

She laughed so hard that tears came to her eyes. "Okay, okay, you win. I couldn't even talk about it, much less write it. I forgot about the clothes, too. Robin's-egg blue! Oh!"

Paul laughed so hard with her that their coffees jiggled on the table. He polished off the rest of his cup.

"Listen to me. This stuff we do comes from here." His voice was suddenly serious as he motioned toward his torso.

Maxine looked at the tight, trim six-pack waist behind his hand and nearly shuddered.

"From your gut, from experience. Write it from here, Maxine. Any time you can't, then stop, put your pen down for the day, and pick it back up when you are ready to be honest and have confession with the paper. Treat it like Holy Communion—with reverence. If you can't tell it right, skip that section and go to something else, but don't half step. Your readers will out you, and will rightfully call you on it."

She let her gaze find a point in the center of the table. If he was writing from passion when he did that second book of his . . . Goodness gracious, she couldn't go there. "Paul, I don't know. I'm writing this for *my kids*. Jesus."

"Like their mommy and daddy never had a life, and they fell off the back of the turnip truck? Give it to them when they're older, then." Mischief filled his voice, and he winked at her. "Why shouldn't they know how much their parents loved each other? And how hard it was for them to do the right thing, or sneak to do the wrong thing?" Paul Gotier chuckled and toyed with his mug. "They were obviously conceived in love. And from what you left out, one can only assume, within a lot of passion."

"Yeah, but . . . Even if they are sixty when I die, I wouldn't want my kids to . . . oh, God!"

"Maxine." All teasing was gone from his tone. "Just do it as elegantly as you've done the other difficult subjects. You do not have to exploit the other person. You don't have to tell when you lost your virginity, or how, or anything like that. Stick with what this book is about—the feelings. Tell the readers what you felt like after that first kiss—not the details of it. Explain how much it relaxed you to know Kenny wasn't pressuring you. These are good lessons for both your daughters and your son. And I forgot to mention how much I respected the way you handled other people's business in your work."

Her vision became blurry. This man had read her work and saw what was in it, what she was trying to do. She now had language to wrap around what had been missing at home. Paul gave her time to think, process, describe, and come to conclusions through easy conversation. He respected the communication process, and didn't force the exchange into roles that felt distinctly female or male—it just was.

She picked at her napkin, thinking about all the feelings she'd kept inside. No one had ever heard her, really. They didn't know what the family peacemaker, the family voice of reason, felt or thought during times of crisis. Not even her sisters, really. All they knew was that Maxine was the level-headed one, Maxine kept her cool, saw all sides of the story, and knew what to do. What if her sisters and the rest of the family had been wrong? What if for just once, she did something rash, or didn't have the right answers?

"I never really thought what I had to say was all that special, so I only talked about what was important to other people." She kept her gaze toward the window, feeling too exposed to do otherwise.

"Maxine, you have a regal voice that should be heard. Like when you spoke of your sister's divorce— you didn't go into all the harrowing details of it. That's no one's business but hers. But you talked about what it did to you to see her so upset, and how her hurt pierced you. You talked about how afraid her crisis made you for her, for yourself. *That's* elegant writing. Graceful and gracious."

She sniffed and swallowed hard. If he didn't stop, she was going to slide out of her chair into a puddle on the floor. "You said it needed a hook and an end, though. I stopped writing a few years ago, and I just don't know how."

"What is the greatest conflict, or obstacle, or lesson you want to convey to your children?"

Paul leaned forward, his beautiful hands making a tent over his empty coffee mug as he intently waited for her answer.

"I don't want my children to be afraid to embrace change, or to grow, no matter where they are in their stage of life—but I also don't want them to forget their roots, or what's important. And I want them to know it's okay not to know what to do . . . and that they have the right to be afraid—even terrified, at times . . . and it's okay to share that dark truth with someone. I also want them to have a solid connection of faith to keep them going when all else fails." Maxine let her breath out hard with relief. She hadn't even known that's where the story or tale was headed, until he made her stop and think about it, and actually speak the words.

"Then take them on the journey, Maxine. This story tells of a woman's journey—but her passage through the ordinary and seemingly mundane is extraordinary, because she has balanced the old with the new with dignity, grace, and honor. Her struggle is a universal one."

His gaze left hers, and he was doodling on his napkin, sketching nothing, his ink just making marks.

"This is a story that could have mass appeal, because it's about life as one knew it, but with time eroding what was, and replacing that with new paradigms. The average person can relate to what you've written, Maxine, because we all struggle with frustrations, pressures, and have a bit of nostalgia within us. And we all want to do the right thing, to raise our children the way we remember the elders seemed to—which looked so effortless at the time, but which we've come to learn required great sacrifice, the half of which we'll probably never know. Saying that you have stumbled, been afraid, not known the way, but *made* a way out of no way, is a wonderful gift to give your children. A glimpse into their mother's life, told from a loving place in her heart, so they might not make the same mistakes she did, or so that they might do the same right things she did. It's masterful in its simplicity."

He glanced up and held her with a tender expression. "Maxine, you have a potential best-seller. Tell your story. And keep it real. We have all been afraid and not known what to do about a situation. How are you going to end this story?"

They sat in silence, his question thick in the air between them, laden with overtones they both seemed to quietly understand.

"I don't know," she finally whispered.

"I've given you a lot to think about, and you have about fifty pages to go, to get your story to manuscript length—with only three full weeks left in class."

Maxine just nodded. "I know. Any suggestions?"

"I think the main character in your story is in the midst of one of the greatest struggles of her life. It's a private struggle between the known and the unknown, right and wrong, what she's been taught and what she wants to do—and I think this woman never thought she'd find herself in such a predicament." Paul looked away. "Sometimes you have to let the novel breathe. Give it a rest. Work on the known areas for next week and see where the characters themselves take you."

Maxine nodded, incapable of speaking. The man had made the sexiest, most totally suave pass at her that she'd ever experienced, but had remained a gentleman. Everything that he'd said to her could have been taken two ways—only his eyes and the expression on his face underscored his true meaning. Watching him watch her, and also fight with his impulses, made a pure sizzle of power and fear run through her. The silent undertow beneath his surface of restraint pulled at her until her toes practically curled in her shoes.

"I need to go home now," she whispered. "It's late, and . . ."

He nodded, not making her finish her retreat. "Yes. That would be best."

eight

What was she going to do?

Maxine dropped her front door keys twice before she could get her hands to stop shaking enough to manage the locks. *Please, let Kenny be asleep.* She had to get herself together before she walked into her house.

As soon as she walked in the front door, she froze. Kenny was sitting on the sofa, soft music was playing, the lights were low, candles were burning, and flowers were on the coffee table. Oh, no. This wasn't right. She needed a second. Some space.

"Hi," he said in a pleasant voice. "How was class?"

"Oh, uh, class? Class was fine. Just fine," she said fast, snatching off her jacket and fumbling to get it to stay on the hook. She dropped her pocketbook, scooped it up, and flung it in a nearby armchair with her portfolio.

"Come sit down, then. Talk to me."

She stared at her husband. *Talk to me? Oh, Lord, you know I have sinned in my mind, and you are torturing me.*

Maxine took her time moving toward the sofa. The pink carnations her husband had brought made her cover her mouth. He smiled at her, and tears came to her eyes. She was so out of order, had been so wrong, heaven help her. She sat down on the edge of the couch and took a deep breath to steady herself.

"These are really pretty, Kenny. Thank you."

"Well, I thought about some of the stuff you said, and I haven't been hearing you, I guess . . . and uh, I made the kids lunch for tomorrow, 'cause I didn't see any bags in the fridge. I miss you, Maxine."

She closed her eyes and nodded. "Thank you, honey." She wanted to weep. Half of her wanted to just hug him and have a good, old-fashioned cry because he'd finally started to come around, while the other half of her wanted to wail because his efforts were feeling like too little, too late. Guilt stabbed her conscience. Three weeks ago, she would have floated away on cloud nine. But three weeks into this struggle, and with much water under the bridge, she was watching his relationship repair job like a spectator from a strange, out-of-body experience.

"Why are you sitting so far away? C'mon over here, and tell me about your class."

She looked at her husband's eyes, and the way they searched her face. She saw both fear, and want, and apology . . . but for some strange reason, she wasn't ready to just go back to the familiar and make love to him. Something very fragile had snapped inside her, and she had changed.

"There's not much to tell," she hedged. "We all brought in our passages, and workshopped together, and critiqued each other's writing. We all have to redraft our stuff for next week and polish it."

It was obvious that Kenny wasn't totally following

the process, which was all right. What was important was that he was making an effort to understand her world. But rather than stay in this uncomfortable gray zone, she opted for the tried and true. "So how was your day today?"

"You know . . . our son is a pretty awesome kid. He's worried about us, that things could get strained again for a long time, like they did before. But I told him that this time his dad wasn't gonna make the same dumb mistakes."

She stared at her husband for a moment. Renewed guilt lacerated her. Kenny wasn't being bought off by the old standard line, and it suddenly dawned on her how much she used that as a defense mechanism. When she didn't feel like talking, she simply shifted gears so she could be a spectator. Ahmad had even gone to his father, trying to get in the middle of things to help. Now she *really* wanted to cry, but she forced a smile and nodded.

"I know I'm not good at the academics, Maxine, and maybe that's why I stay on the kids about it—but I really respect people who are . . . like you, my wife. I don't know why I felt so . . . I don't know. I just didn't like the whole idea at first, but that wasn't right. I just want you to know I respect you, okay?"

"I respect you, too, baby . . . and love you a lot." She did, and hoped that he could hear all that she meant by the statement. For the first time in her life, she could identify with male evasion of the facts—some things, one just didn't bring home. Some things were better left unsaid. He was being a friend, an involved, communicative partner, and now she was the one with a lot of mess with her. "But enough about me . . . how was your day?"

She needed something to divert the conversation away from writing, her class, or her professor. It was ironic, how all this time she'd wanted him to embrace her art, and now she wanted to just keep that to herself. She had to—the situation was too charged. Maxine settled back against the sofa and allowed Kenny's arm to drape over her shoulders.

"Same ole, same ole," he sighed after a moment. "Maybe that's another part of my problem with all of this."

They sat for a while just listening to the music together, each painfully aware that they no longer had much beyond the kids and the household to share.

"Things going all right at the garage?" It was her attempt to break through the invisible barrier, and she was curious to learn what, beyond Ahmad's words, had changed Kenny's approach. What had her son said that had affected Kenny like this? Now she was really worried.

"Yeah, Maxine. You know not much breaks the routine down there. Trucks are holding up. Shorty called out, but that's also normal." He shrugged, and stroked Maxine's arm. "How was your private critique session?"

Kenny's question seemed to leap out of the blue. Growing wary and defensive, she picked at her fingernails.

"Oh, you know. I've got a *lot* of work to do to make my manuscript tight. Gotier really marked it. Looks like a Catholic school nun got a hold of it with a red pen." She tried to sound nonchalant as her husband gave her his undivided attention.

"Well, from what they say, he's one of the best."

Maxine nodded, but glanced at her husband from

the side of her eye. What did Kenny know about "what they say"?

"Good-looking, single man like that, he probably doesn't have a lot of time to be marking people's work up, so it must mean he thinks you're good—or likes you, or something."

Maxine's jaw went slack. Her husband was *jealous.* Noooo. . . .

"How do you know what the man looks like?"

Kenny glanced away and kept his focus on the flowers. "I read, from time to time . . . newspapers and magazines and stuff, when the garage isn't busy. Figured since you were in class with somebody I didn't know about, then I should get to know more about him."

Maxine let her breath out in a weary sigh. "So the flowers, the music, doing the lunches, all that is because you read the *Essence* article, isn't it? It's not really because of anything Ahmad was worried about or spoke to you about, or that you picked up on for yourself?"

When he didn't reply, she stood up.

"Maxine, where are you going?"

"To bed. I'm tired."

"But wait." Kenny now stood, too. "We never get to talk anymore. Or do anything else, for that matter."

"Kenny . . . You still don't get it, do you?" Her tone was compassionate, because for the very first time, she understood that he really didn't. The realization made her sad, and it created a level of fatigue within her that she couldn't explain. "I wanted you to find an interest in my work, but not because someone forced you, not because you felt there was some imminent threat, and not because you wanted to placate me. I wanted you to *want* to talk to me, and share things with me. . . . I don't know why. . . . In fact, I don't even know where I'm headed with this conversation."

She turned on her heels and slowly walked up the stairs.

"Lem, man, can we grab a beer?"

"Yeah, Kenny." Lem yawned. "You know what time it is, though?"

"I know. But right now, I could really use a beer between brothers."

"Aw'right. Let me tell Bird I'm going out, and I'll meet you at the spot in twenty minutes. Cool?"

"Yeah. That's cool. Thanks."

Lem stared at the telephone when Kenny hung up, as Bird propped herself up on one elbow in bed.

"Baby, that was Kenny."

"What's the matter?"

"I don't know, but he sounded shook up."

"Kenny?"

"Wants to go have a beer, now, this late on a Wednesday night."

"Oh, shit. I'd better call Maxine."

"No. Don't. Let me find out what's messed with Kenny's head like this, first. Kenny *never* asks for advice or wants to talk, but it was in his voice, Bird."

She stared at him, nervously covering her mouth with her hand.

"I know, baby. This is serious, because Kenny wasn't even yelling or fussing He just said he needed to talk, more or less."

"Oh my God . . . what did my sister do?"

* * *

"Hey, man," Lem said, as upbeat as he could, and then slid into the open barstool next to Kenny. "So, what's up?"

Kenny just stared into his beer for a moment. "I don't know how, but I think I just lost my wife."

"What?" Lem waved away the bartender who was approaching to take his order. He didn't want a drink. He needed info on a clear head, first.

"I saw the magazine," Kenny muttered. "Read the article. This guy is something. When I ignored my wife, he found her hanging out there like a diamond."

"Aw, now, Kenny, c'mon." Now Lem motioned aggressively for bar service. Screw a beer; this was a whiskey kinda night. "You know Maxine isn't like that. She loves you and would never do anything to shake up the household—*like that*. Not with her children there, too. Naw." Lem adamantly shook his head. "Naw. Don't even go there. You're making yourself crazy."

"Wish I could be sure." Kenny took a swig of his beer. "I read that whole magazine, in fact. It went into about how women think. What they find sexy in a man. What pisses them off, hurts their feelings, and all that kind of stuff. I scored real low, on all counts. The sad part of it was, it was crap I've been doing for years without knowing it. Then I read about Gotier, and shit—his game isn't just tight, Lem. It's awesome."

Lem accepted his drink from the bartender and sipped it slowly. "Yeah but like we were saying at dinner, what good is some man who can't do anything but write some fancy—"

"The man used to be a carpenter. His father was a

craftsman from St. Lucia, and you know those folks from the islands can do some labor. Best union men in town." Kenny let his breath out with disgust. "Built his own house down there with his bare hands. Gotta give credit where credit is due."

Lem held his drink midair for a moment. "No shit," he murmured. "But still. Maxine is another story. She's different from the women he's used to."

"That's just it. The man claims to have been celibate while raising his two young sons and looking for Ms. Right. He got spiritual, and started—"

"See, now see, there's a problem. He's a religious fanatic, Kenny. Maxine isn't hardly going to turn her household upside down for someone that deep into the church to the point where he's stayed *celibate*. That ain't natural." Lem sloshed his glass against Kenny's mug, appearing vindicated.

"Lem," Kenny said patiently, too weary to fight. "He doesn't sleep with just any woman, because he doesn't want his sons to do it. He's trying to set an example for his little boys."

"Is he gay, or what?"

"Not if you read the excerpt from his book."

The two men stared at each other.

"You read the excerpt, man?"

"Yeah."

"Why'd you do that to yourself?" Lem sighed, and focused his gaze on the liquor in his glass.

Kenny finished his beer and ordered another one. "We're not connecting anymore. She doesn't have anything to say, other than good morning or good night. She laughs with other people . . . and clams up when I come around. Dresses in sweatpants and T-shirts for me, and gets all dolled up to go to class."

"Well, man . . . she's going out of the house to a class. Don't let her wearing something nice to go out shake your confidence. I mean, it's not like she's wearing club gear, right?"

No," Kenny murmured. "She just looks beautiful and radiant and excited . . . until she approaches me."

Lem let his breath out in exasperation. "Well, did you buy her some flowers?"

Kenny nodded. "And she hardly noticed them. I even put on the classics and lit a candle, and she said she was tired."

Lem just stared at him. "This is serious," he whispered.

"I know." Kenny's gaze settled on the row of bottles behind the bar. "She's never been like this before—not for this long."

"How long is this long?"

"About a month," Kenny murmured, downing the remainder of his beer. The admission tore at his soul in a very fragile place within it.

"You've gotta fix this, man. Immediately, if not sooner."

"I didn't start it, and—"

"Doesn't matter who started it, Kenny. Does it?" Lem looked at him hard. "You've got everything to lose, and this Gotier has everything to gain, if you don't turn this around."

"I don't know how." His voice was a rough whisper, and he motioned to the bartender as he swallowed hard. "I never had to compete for Maxine before, not even in high school . . . never figured I had to as her husband."

"Well, okay. Let's be rational here. It's not like he's made a play for her—and if he's all religious and whatnot, then he probably won't."

"He took her for a solo cup of coffee," Kenny grumbled, unable to look at Lem. His pride was in tatters, and his ego beyond crushed. What the hell was he doing in a bar confessing to his brother-in-law? The only thing he hadn't said was how deeply wounded he was when Maxine told him he was no longer her friend.

"Coffee. Alone?"

Kenny could only nod.

"No, man. That's highly out of order."

"Well, I don't get a vote on this. The ladies have—"

"Uh, uh, Kenny. No. I'm not having Bird be involved as a coconspirator. No."

"Nothing we can do about this. I don't know why I even brought it up. Guess I just needed to say it out loud, so I could deal with it."

"You've just gotta get a plan, man. You need to win back Maxine's attention—that's all."

Kenny stared at his best male friend, then slumped his shoulders in defeat. "Maxine is my wife, Lem. She's the love of my life. And if she's sick of being married and doesn't want to be with me anymore, I can't force her to change. Some things, you just have to accept."

Lem shook his head. "Just promise me that you'll go out swinging. If it were Bird, I'd fight for her. Period."

Kenny downed his beer and stood. "That's because you're still young. Wait a few more years, and all the fight'll be out of you."

* * *

She'd worked like a demon all week on arranging and rearranging her prose. Feeling satisfied that she'd gone to the next level with it, she printed off a clean copy and left Paul Gotier's marked version next to the laptop in the kitchen. Maxine paused and printed off a second clean copy. This way she could bring in the revision with the edited version, and have one left at home to tinker with. That man wrote notes like a doctor's prescription—practically illegible, she thought with a chuckle. She couldn't wait to show him what she'd accomplished.

It didn't matter to her that the chores in the household had slipped this week. It was just one week out of fifty-two; her family would survive. At least Kenny had stopped complaining. He was floating around like a ghost, but staying out of her way. Her sisters seemed to have become unusually quiet, which was a good thing, because she certainly didn't have time to talk about her behavior.

In fact, it was all good. For the first time in her life, she'd had time to come up with solutions to her writing problems, and to really learn. Mrs. Jenkins, Bird's babysitter for little Jay, had been a godsend by agreeing to watch her baby girl, too, this week.

Maxine gathered up her papers and paced across the room. She couldn't wait to see Paul's expression when he read her revisions. Class, as usual, would be great—but coffee, alone, with his full attention, would be perfect.

It wasn't until Kenny got through the door and remembered that Maxine was in class, and his children were at Teri's house, that he really saw the clutter. While filled with children, voices, and general chaos, their house had seemed to be as it always was: fairly neat, but definitely well lived in. Tonight, however, it looked abandoned.

Defeat claimed him. Something had begun to splinter and fray within their relationship . . . he wasn't sure how far back. His household and his marriage were hemorrhaging, and he couldn't seem to find out how to fix it.

He walked through the living room, past the dead dining room, and into a kitchen where no food was waiting. Nothing but a silent computer and a pile of pages. Kenny retrieved a beer from the refrigerator and opened it with a twist, then flipped the cap onto the table with his thumb and forefinger, the way they used to pitch bottle tops when they were kids. He sat heavily in the chair opposite what used to be Maxine's and watched the cap spiral around the table, stuttering to a wobbly stop—just like their relationship had, he thought. Maybe his son had been right: Maxine just wanted to feel appreciated, and he'd taken too long to show it.

He looked at the still cap that rested against Maxine's pages. He brought the cold beer to his lips, took a deep swig with his eyes closed, and sighed after he'd swallowed. The icy emulsion felt good going down, but an added flavor of salt covered his tongue. Kenny swallowed again and blinked back the moisture in his eyes.

He would have read her work, if he knew it meant so much to her. He just never realized. His hand reached across the table to the stack of paper. He loved her voice, didn't she know that? He loved her laughter, how could she not know? He loved the way she cooked, and made a home . . . and God in heaven knew she was the only woman he'd ever wanted to have his children with. He missed her touch so much some nights, he almost couldn't breathe.

Kenny fingered the pages with reverence as his gaze held onto them. How could a pile of paper mean more to her than all of them . . . more than him? What was in these pages? As he began to read, he found himself shaking his head in agreement, laughing out loud, and sniffing away a hard memory as he heard Maxine's voice come alive inside his mind.

"Oh, yeah . . . I remember that," he whispered into the empty kitchen, his voice seeming to echo off the walls. He laughed as she described the house party that they'd sneaked to, then became very quiet when he read how their first kiss made her feel.

Kenny closed his eyes. His wife had put the most important things to her soul down on paper, and he had never read it. He'd stupidly opened the door to his wife's heart, to allow another man to enter . . . just because that man listened. He might just as well open his front door and take his family on vacation—and have the gall to be surprised if his home was robbed.

Kenny slid the stack back to where he'd found it and glanced at the kitchen wall clock. He'd been sitting there for hours, and had only gotten a little more than halfway through. Time was playing tricks on him—hours had flown by and seemed like minutes, just like years had flown by and seemed like yesterday.

While he wanted to read more, to know more about Maxine's view of the world, he wanted more than any-thing to find his wife, to stake his claim and pull her into his arms. This woman was worth fighting for.

And that's just what he was gonna do.

"Maxine . . . I don't know what to say," Paul murmured, his hands filled with her papers.

"Is that bad or good?" she teased, having grown comfortable in his presence over the weeks, but still insecure about her writing.

He looked up from reading and set her work down carefully beside his mug at the diner table. His intense gaze almost made the air crackle and pop around him.

"This work is so improved," he said in a quiet voice. "You have captured that difficult section and handled it with aplomb."

Maxine sighed and smiled, and took a sip of her coffee. "Now I can breathe."

But Paul wasn't laughing, nor was he smiling. Uh-oh . . .

"I'm glad you can, because I'm barely breathing right now, Maxine."

Maxine nearly dropped her mug. She didn't know how to respond. The man had just come right out and said it.

"I'm sorry," he murmured. "It might have been the truth, but it was way out of line."

Still stunned, she said nothing.

"It was my fault," he joked, gathering her papers up and awkwardly straightening them. "I told you to be honest, to tell it from your gut. Whew."

She was flattered beyond speech. Her writing had that effect?

Paul held her in an intense stare and nodded as

though he'd read her mind. "Truth is some powerful juju, lady."

For a moment they just looked at each other, and then laughed together.

"I'm flattered," she finally said. "That the master of words really thinks this is good. For real, Paul. Thanks for the confidence boost."

"I have something for you," he said, all mirth leaving his voice. "Nothing big, or inappropriate . . . but I saw it and thought of you."

Now she was worried. This wasn't innocent flirting; this had gone to the next level. "I . . . uh . . ." Her brain scrambled for something rational, sensible, to say, but came away blank as he dug in his pocket and produced a tiny charm.

"It's a lock adornment for good luck. Hetheru—the Egyptian patron goddess of the arts."

Maxine studied the small silver figure, which was exquisite, and intricately sculpted. Sitting in the center of his outstretched palm as an offering, it called to her. Her forefinger touched it, but she didn't pick it up. She just toyed with it in the center of Paul's palm for a moment before withdrawing her hand.

"It's beautiful," she murmured, "but I can't accept it. It wouldn't be right."

"Lean forward," he commanded, his voice firm and gentle as he reached for her hair. He softly traced her cheek, found the stray lock that always came away from her ponytail, and began to clip the jewelry to it.

His finger had left a burning trail down the side of her face, and she could smell his earthy, natural scent as his hands worked so close to her cheek. It took all of her strength not to turn in to those broad, open palms.

"There. A goddess for a goddess. All is right in the universe now."

"Paul . . . this isn't right, and you know it. I'm married."

There, she'd finally said it. He nodded, but didn't retrieve the figure from her hair.

"I know," he finally said.

Maxine picked at the edge of her napkin. "Then . . . Well . . . But, why me?"

"Are you crazy, Maxine?"

He seemed shocked.

"I'm sitting here with a beautiful woman who is so sensitive and honest that she takes my breath away—has for weeks." Paul covered her hand for a moment, and then withdrew it to hold onto his mug. "Maxine, the moment you bumped into me in that classroom, I was blown away."

"Now I have to ask you if *you're* the one who's crazy. I almost knocked a steaming cup of coffee all over you. What an introduction."

Paul chuckled. "Yeah, you did. And you were so real . . . so down-to-earth, and so nervous that it did something to me. Do you have any idea how many false people I run into every waking minute of my life?"

She searched his eyes for fraud, but found none. There was a wistful honesty about his tone, and she'd never even considered that he might be lonely.

"All you wanted, when you came through my class-room door, was to learn. You came in there without pretense, with a lot of humility, and your eyes were searching for knowledge, Maxine. There was something so pure in you that I haven't seen in so long, I—" He glanced away. "Suffice to say that it swayed me."

"But I didn't mean to give the impression that . . . Paul—"

He put his fingers to his lips. The simple gesture made her lose her trend of thought.

"I don't go around the country picking up women, married or otherwise. And you didn't do anything to try to lead me down this path, Maxine. That's what is so magnetic about you—you were just being yourself." He shook his head. "Haven't you read your own work? Don't you know what you project?"

"I shouldn't have—well, I didn't want my work to, uh . . . That wasn't my actual intent."

She was babbling. He was smiling. Oh, Lord help her. This man was making her forget she was married.

"Maxine. Read your own work from an objective point of view. You are sensitive, caring, and run deeper than still waters." His voice was like a whisper, stroking her insides. "Baby, you're honest."

He took a slow breath in through his nose and let it out of his mouth. She almost shuddered at the way he was trying to collect himself. He'd called her "baby," and he'd crooned the word in that accent that was making her dizzy.

"But, but, I . . ."

"Everything you believe in and hold dear is what I've been looking for in a woman all my life—and with my lifestyle, I have yet to find it. I listened to the way you talked about your kids, your husband, the things you do on a daily basis to make a household a home. And for a man who has been to hell and back in his own home, that is the most seductive, sensual unveiling one can imagine."

He took a sip of his coffee and swallowed it hard. All she could do was stare at him.

"So, Maxine, you are correct. I'm out of line, totally wrong in every biblical sense, and probably out of my mind for even being so honest. But I thought you had the right to know two things. Number one; I am helping you with your work because it's deserving, my attraction to you notwithstanding. Number two; I find you compelling as a woman—beautiful on the outside, as well as on the inside, which is a rare quality. And if your husband ever takes you for granted and acts like a swine, I would be more than willing to take his cast-off pearls—permanently."

"Oh, my God." The words had fallen out of her mouth before she could stop them.

Paul chuckled and calmly sipped his coffee. "So, how are you going to finish your book?"

Maxine blinked, stunned. "The book?"

"Yeah. The book. How is it going to end?"

"I can't leave Kenny . . . I can't leave my kids. I can't just up and do something like that!"

"I know," Paul murmured. "You just needed to know that for sure."

Now she was pissed off. "So you were just playing with me?" She was about to stand when his palm slid up her forearm.

"No. I wasn't playing. I just think I've gained a little insight into this woman who I won't be able to forget. I didn't think she was the type of woman to leave her home of thirteen years. But I had to make sure."

Flushed, she looked away. Paul Gotier had no idea just how dangerously close to the edge she'd been teetering, but he was right. She wasn't leaving home.

Paul reached into his wallet and pulled out a business card. "I'm going to write the name of my agent on the back of this—and when you finish your book, I'd appreciate a final copy of it."

"Of course I'd send you a copy of it," she whispered.

He wasn't looking at her as he scribbled information on the back of it. "Tell him that I said to submit your work to him. You'll also find my private home number in St. Lucia here, as well as several other places you can track me down." Paul glanced up, his expression serious. "Maxine. I wasn't playing at all. If you ever change your mind, call me. This is my personal address, not the general one for the public. This is yours only. Understood?"

Maxine nodded and closed the card within her palm. "Thank you for the agent's number." she whispered. "And for understanding, and not being . . . not taking it . . . you know what I mean?"

"Yeah, I do," he said quietly, enfolding her hands within his. "And it's the nicest, most gracious retreat I've ever been given." He chuckled, making her smile. "I might have to write this out of my system, though, Maxine."

Her eyes widened, and it seemed to make him chuckle harder. He let her hands go, picked up his coffee, and raked his fingers through his locks.

"Might have to do a story about how I got my mind blown by a married woman . . . a sexy, tall Chicago woman who was as sweet as pie and as fiery as the sun, and who made a grown man act crazy—made dis island man wanna work juju to get her. But couldn't, 'cause she was a Christian woman, a mother at dat."

She could tell he'd deepened his accent to make her smile, and she chuckled.

"This story might have to go to the grave with me, Paul."

"Aiyree. This is why I said that we only know half of what our elders went through. Old ladies rocking on the porch laugh to themselves for no reason sometimes. Old men chuckle and shake their heads, and then pick up the conversation where they left off. This is the stuff of legends—the untold stories, yes?"

"Paul," she murmured, "I'll be rocking on my back porch about this for a long time. The untold story about how a wonderful, kind, attractive, and honorable man made me feel like a woman again, without putting a hand on me." She held his gaze within her own. "And I'll write in my mind about how he made me put things into perspective, into context . . . but his passing through will always make me wonder what might have happened, under different circumstances."

Silence enveloped them for a moment, then Paul nodded to break the trance.

"Might have to 'splain to da pages, myself, 'bout how that lean Chicago girl kept me up at night tryin' to bargain wit me Jesus for her to step wrong wit me, and how I'da taken her and all her children wherever she wanted to go. Might have to tell how she could write her natural pretty butt off, and how she burned me to an ember, sitting in a damned diner, drinking coffee, reading about how passionate she really was inside. Den, I might hafta tell 'bout how it was me own foolishness, 'cause that woman had integrity—and told me to my face she wasn't leaving the man from her story. Which I already knew better than to hope, but it does spring eternal—like Ja."

"Thank you so much, Paul." Her voice was a quaky whisper.

"Now me soul mate is gonna tell me to quit before she cries, 'cause her pretty heart is so loving, she cares." He patted her hand. "That's her beauty."

His accent faded and he continued in a low voice, "Kenneth Chadway is a lucky man. Go home to him. Finish your book, and send it to my agent. Promise me at least that much."

"I'll finish it. I promise," she said, loosening the amulet from her lock. "But I can't wear this. Not in Kenny's home, not to bed with him, not in my house."

Paul opened his palm and accepted the trinket. "No. A woman like you couldn't." He placed the little silver goddess next to his coffee mug and stared at it. "I'm going to take a page out of your book, Professor Maxine. Gonna name my leading lady Hetheru—and you'll know who I'm talking about. And I'm going to do it from a man's perspective: what goes on inside his head when he wants what he can't have, but is old enough to understand why—without drama. I'll preserve your dignity, that I promise."

"You were serious? You're actually going to write this?" Maxine covered her mouth with her hand.

He laughed a deep, cleansing, resounding laugh. "Yes, Maxine. I came here all dried up for ideas. I was tapped out, emotionally exhausted from touring, deadlines, and taking care of two little boys. And for the first time in years, I got to relive that first book passion . . . and share it with a marvelous friend. Thank you so much, Maxine. You lit a fire in a lot of places within me. Not just the obvious. You also taught me how important it is to catalog those memories, but to do so in a way that does not tell other's people's business—just your own. That's the only part of the story that one owns—your head talk, not someone else's."

"I taught you something?" Her mouth was hanging open, but she couldn't close it.

"Wasn't that the first thing I told you? The teacher always walks away from a classroom schooled." He glanced at her hands. "Go home, Mrs. Chadway, before I say something else over the line . . . like, I won't forget you. For a couple of more weeks in class, we can hang and let this remain where it should—on the straight and narrow."

She stood, barely able to keep her balance. Out of deep appreciation she kissed his cheek, and then wiped it away with the tips of her fingers. He just closed his eyes and drew in a long breath.

"Thank you," she whispered again. She had to get out of there.

Kenny had seen all he needed to see. His wife was laughing all cozy with that Gotier guy in the plate-glass window of the diner. He had touched her hand, had touched her hair, and they both were sitting there like they were ready to sop each other up with a biscuit. His first impulse had been to just barge in there and turn over the table—but if Maxine wanted a divorce, if she wanted their marriage to be over, he wasn't going to be her prison warden.

Never in a million years could anyone have told him his marriage would end like this.

nine

She'd never wanted to get home so badly in her life. She needed to walk through the door and get grounded.

Total elation at still being found attractive enough to make a man proposition her—not just any man, but a man like Paul Gotier—shot adrenaline through her entire nervous system. After thirteen years, a new man had sat across from her, leaning in close, trying to seduce her, a mother of three. A gentleman, too. A man of principle, an intellectual, a friend. Wow! One who had almost begged her to run away with him—kids included. Outrageous! Delicious. Insanely passionate.

At the same time, she had broken through the quandary within her own spirit to realize just how much she was still in love with her husband. Paul Gotier was so intense, and had so many wonderful qualities . . . he'd just plain old opened her damned nose, is what he did. But oddly, that made her want to go home. She wanted to feel that way with Kenny. It was as if the reminder that her body could feel that way, that her soul could catch fire like that, sparked the memory of what they'd shared for so long.

And nothing was perfect. If she did go with Paul, sooner or later, she'd discover his demons and foibles. No human being walked the planet flawless. Her husband was a great lover, a good father, and a wonderful husband—in general. He didn't need to be a literary aficionado, too. She plain old liked the way he smelled when he came home from work.

She loved her home, too—that noisy, chaotic center of gravity that kept things real. Her children, oh my God, what would she do if something crazy happened, and their spirits and minds were scarred? Never. Not by her own hand.

Maxine pulled the car to a stop in her the driveway next to Kenny's truck and jumped out, grabbing her portfolio and purse with impatience. Tonight, Kenny was coming to bed with her. Tonight, they could laugh and cry and apologize for all the silly mess between them. Tonight it didn't matter if he ever read her work or not. She'd been validated outside herself, and carried that brand inside her soul—so there was no reason to upset her happy home.

She eagerly turned the keys in the locks and glanced around the dark living room. She could have sworn she left a light on inside. Could the bulbs have blown?

"Kenny?" she called out softly, closing the door behind her.

"Yeah," a voice said from the darkened living room chair.

"Why are you sitting in the dark?" She chuckled, shaking her head as she walked nearer to switch on the light.

"I needed to think about what I was going to say to you. Leave it off and sit down," he commanded.

Maxine stopped mid-step. She'd never heard him like this before, only when there was a death in the family. She covered her mouth with her hand and let it drop to her chest.

"Oh, my God, Kenny. The children—"

"Yeah, the children, Maxine."

"What happened!" Ignoring his instructions, she raced toward where he was seated and flicked on the light, and immediately sat across from him on the ottoman. His tone was so calm that she knew it had to be a disaster. He couldn't even look her in the eyes, and his face seemed puffed and red, like he'd been crying. Her children . . .

"It was the hardest thing I've ever had to see in my life," he murmured. "Never thought it would happen to our family."

Her heart was beating so fast, it made her ears ring.

"Kenny, Kenny—no matter how bad it is, you have to tell me what happened. *Now.*"

She leaned forward to reach for his hands, and he snatched them away from her.

"Do *not* touch me. Not after what I saw."

He'd sprung up from his chair so fast that she toppled backward on the ottoman, and she had to brace herself to keep from falling to the floor. Her mind quickly realigned itself. This was no death tragedy. This was pure, unadulterated rage. This was a place where she'd never seen Kenneth Chadway go, at least not in her direction. This was a possible "call 911" kind of husband fury. Maxine became very, very still as she watched her husband pace, breathing hard, tears threatening his eyes.

"How long has this bullshit with Paul Gotier been going on?"

She blinked twice, not believing her ears.

When she took too long to respond, Kenny whirled on her, pointing toward his chest and leaning down in her face.

"I was at the diner, Maxine! I came there to see about my wife, to tell her I was sorry, to try to make amends—and instead, I roll up on some stranger playing with my wife's hair, holding her hands. Are you crazy, Maxine!"

Her eyes felt like the corners of them were splitting, they were open so wide.

"It's not what it looked like, Kenny. Really, honey. There's a whole lot more to the—"

"Not what the *hell* it looked like?"

Maxine scrambled to her feet and crossed the room. She had to think, get this right, explain with some edits—but let Kenny know she'd been straight.

"No," she said as calmly as possible. "It's not what it looked like."

She watched him walk in a circle, praying as he passed each photo and lamp. She knew something was going to probably get thrown or broken. *Please, not my mama's silver frame. No, baby, not the lamp.*

"Kenny, you need to calm down so we can talk about this rationally."

His fist came down like thunder on the mantelpiece, rattling everything on it. "How long, Maxine, were you going to play me for a fool? Huh? How long were you and the 'professor' there going to act like you were in class every Wednesday night!"

"Oh, now see, you have just gone too far, Kenneth Chadway." Her hands were on her hips. This man had lost his damned mind, accusing her like that. Her indignation took some of the wind out of his storm, and she went for broke in the lull.

"So now I'm running around, Kenny? All because you saw me having a cup of coffee with my teacher in a diner? Oh, like if I were having an affair, I'd just tell you where I'd be, and be there? That just makes all the sense in the world." She paced as her ire gained momentum. "Like you didn't want a chance to explain when you were in a shaky predicament that wasn't your fault?"

She knew she had him when he looked away and mumbled, "That was different."

"Oh, really? How?"

"You're mixing apples and oranges, Maxine, and you know it!"

"The situations are the same. Somebody in your professional environment proclaimed an interest in you—one that was flattering, but that you had no intention of acting upon. That person had enough grace, and in my case, chivalry, to leave it be and to understand."

Her husband had a nerve; it was the pot calling the kettle black. Though she did understand now just how awful he must have felt for indulging his ego a little when the shoe was on the other foot.

"Didn't seem like 'the professor' was trying to leave it be, if you ask me," Kenny finally retorted.

Cheap shot. Maxine glared hard at Kenny. "All I know is that, in both cases, the intruders to our marriage have left, or are leaving, town forever. Period. End of story. You saw a situation that was being set straight."

"So that makes it all right for some man to run his finger down the side of your face and play with your hair? That makes it okay for him touch my wife's hands?"

Maxine's cheeks burned with anger and guilt. "Like that woman who used to work for you never kissed you? Never brushed invisible lint off your shoulder, never made any contact whatsoever?"

"We are not talking about some historical incident. We are focused on tonight."

"Oh. So that historical fact should just be stricken from the record, like it never happened, and it's okay that you felt a little bit of a rush from the situation. It's okay that maybe you were flattered by it, after not really feeling appreciated at home. And I guess it shouldn't matter that it threatened me, too? Shouldn't care that it hurt my feelings, made me wonder, made me so angry that I could spit nails, but most of all, made me want to weep at the thought that my husband might have found another woman more attractive than me? Oh. I see. What's good for the goose is not good for the gander?"

She folded her arms over her chest, winded, and glared at Kenny. What the hell could he say to that? It was the naked truth.

"That was different. I didn't sashay in public."

"I was sitting at a diner table. Drinking coffee. More could have happened in a private garage after hours than in a public space—but do I get any credit for being in a chaperoned, public environment? Oooohhhh, noooo."

His eyes saw what they saw, his heart felt what it felt, his rage was what it was, but as usual, there was no arguing with Maxine.

"Well, I don't care," he boomed. "I didn't like it, and I'm not having my wife go out of here at night making a public display of herself! I forbid you to take another class with some man that has the hots for you. Period. Case closed."

"You forbid me?" Maxine's head tilted to the side in amazement.

"That's right, Maxine. I'm not playing. I forbid you—and you need to respect that." Kenny made a slicing motion through the air as he said each word; a vein pulsed in his temple.

Maxine began walking in a circle, repeating "forbid me." She was speaking so softly that the repetitive statement sounded like a strange incantation. Kenny was transfixed, his rage giving way to another emotion—worry.

"Now, Maxine," he said, some of the bluster gone out of his tone, "you need to just calm down and put yourself in my shoes. That's all. I didn't like what I saw, and—"

"You forbid me?" she whispered through her teeth. "Like you're my father?" She kept up her insane pacing. "You forbid me, like you don't trust me to finish two more classes without a chaperone?" She stopped. "You forbid me, like I am your property that you can tell what to do? Like I'm a child?"

She walked to the door and snatched her jacket. She needed some fresh air.

"Where are you going?" He stood with his arms folded. "You better not leave this house, Maxine."

Her husband glared at her, but worry reflected from his eyes. He actually thought she was going to fling herself into Paul Gotier's arms? Just flee her house and run to him? Men were *so* stupid!

She didn't say a word, but grabbed her pocketbook. When she attempted to open the door, he flattened his hand against it, barring her exit like she was a suspect. What gave him the right to block her passage, her growth, her dreams? What gave him the right not to hear her for all these years, and to think that was okay!

"We can stand here like this all night if you want—but you are not going out into the street like this, Maxine."

Was this man crazy? Why? Because the first time in his natural-born life, he had something to be jealous about?

"Now I'm a hostage?" She whispered the question with so much lethal venom that Kenny stepped back. "You *forbid* me, a grown woman?"

He swallowed hard. "Maxine, don't do this."

She didn't even look back as she threw open the door, shattering a pane in it.

Teri sat up in bed as someone buzzed her doorbell and pounded on the door like a crazy person. She flung herself out of bed, grabbed her robe, and prepared to evacuate. A fire was the only possible reason for all this. But when she peeped through the hole, she saw Maxine's face.

"What happened, what happened?" Teri tried to grab hold of Maxine as she burst through the door and began sobbing and pacing.

"I couldn't go to Bird's because the children are there, and I don't want them to see me like this—even though I know you have to get up really early in the morning for your trial. I can't go home—"

The end of Maxine's statement came out in a long,

agonized wail. Teri had the cordless phone in one hand while the other stroked Maxine's back.

"Nine-one-one, Bird," Teri commanded. "We've got a sister down, a brother-in-law on the lam, and God knows what else going on. Get over here, and tell Lem to stay put with the children."

Teri stirred her tea slowly, offering Maxine a sip, which she repeatedly refused. "Bring her some more cold compresses for her face, Bird, so she doesn't look like she's been in a heavyweight fight from the tears."

Bird sucked her teeth and went to the sink to bring back a cool, damp towel for Maxine. "This makes no sense, and you know it, Max."

"I'm not going back," Maxine whispered, turning her wedding band around and around on her finger as she studied it. "I'm tired, y'all. No more."

"Are you having a nervous breakdown?" Bird shouted. "You cannot up and leave your husband and children just because you're tired, Maxine. It's just not done."

"I'd never leave my children."

"Baby, you think Paul Gotier is going to take in you and all those children?" Teri asked in a flat, no-nonsense tone.

Maxine stared out of Teri's huge picture window into the starry night. They weren't getting it. This was not about Paul Gotier. She wouldn't traumatize her children like that . . . even though she had an attractive standing offer that she'd *never* disclose to a soul. "I'll just have to rock about this when I get old," she murmured.

"What?" Teri held her back by both arms. "Maxine,

you have to get this man out of your system, and quick. This is not healthy, and it's not fair to Kenny."

The telephone rang, and Bird answered it before anyone else could.

"If it's Kenny, I'm not here."

"Kenny," Bird announced, "Yeah, she's here with me and Teri. Just let her calm down. Yeah, yeah, that's good, right. Uh-huh. You stay with Lem, and ya'll sit down in the kitchen and talk. Right. No. I don't think she's coming home tonight. We love you, too. Bye."

Bird turned to Maxine. "You know that fool loves you, just like you love him."

"He *forbade* me to go to class, like he was my father." Her sisters shared a glance.

"What happened in the diner, Maxine?" Teri's question was terse and no-nonsense, like her mother used to get when she was frustrated.

"You got some wine?" Maxine sighed. "It's a long story."

Lem sat in his own kitchen, stupefied, as he listened to Kenny's tale and watched his brother-in-law turn his wedding band around and around on his finger. He'd already been clued in to both sides of the story—Bird had gone on so long about this situation every night, giving her sister's side of it, and her own remedies, that he had to take a swig of beer to drown his opinion. He let Kenny vent and rail and get it all out, and simply did the only thing he knew to do: pass the man a beer.

Finally, Kenny looked up at him, his eyes weary and bloodshot. "Lem, he was playing in her hair, and she let him."

"No . . ."

"I lie to you not, Lem."

"Damn, man." It was worse than he'd thought. Lem picked at the wet label on his beer. What did you say to a man who'd witnessed something like that? "Maybe Maxine had something in her hair, and he was brushing it out?" The comment was so lame that Lem couldn't even look at Kenny when he'd said it.

"Yeah, right." Kenny took a healthy swig of brew and set the bottle down hard on the table.

Lem nodded. The only response that immediately came to mind was something Bird might say as a retort. And that was easy, since they'd practically been arguing about the hypothetical situation for weeks.

"But that's all that went down, right? Some guy tried to get cozy with Maxine, and she came home."

"Did you hear anything I've said in the last hour?" Kenny sat back, his expression incredulous.

Lem nodded again. "Maxine maybe got herself cornered in a situation that she wasn't sure how to handle."

"That's exactly what happened."

"All right, then," Lem hedged. "You said it yourself. She got into something she couldn't handle—not like she was trying to be sneaky or play you, man. That's not Maxine's way—and probably the reason she couldn't handle it all was because she's *not* a player. Think about it, Kenny."

Lem could tell in the quiet moments that passed that some of what he was saying was getting through.

"Maxine is so naive. That's the thing, man. She doesn't know what's out here, how men really are. That's what I was trying to tell her, before she got that damned computer and lost her mind."

Lem nodded. It was important that Kenny feel like he had an ally. And it was equally important to press the point of his sister-in-law's chastity. If Kenny ever believed that Maxine had crossed the line, there would be no words. Damn, he hated family drama.

"She was where she said she was gonna be, and in a public place—not somewhere off sneaking and creeping." Lem gave Kenny a reassuring glance. "In all likelihood, the guy made a move, and she probably giggled from being so undone and flattered, after thirteen years of never having anything like that happen to her, and she rushed home." Lem took a swig of his beer after calmly stating the facts.

"And all of that is supposed to be all right?"

"No, it's not all right, Kenny."

"Well, that's what I was saying."

"You ask yourself why she was so flattered?" Bird's argument was still lingering in his head, and Lem knew this was the only way to squash the bull once and for all. Kenny had to get it, learn from what happened, and set things right with Maxine, or this nonsense would rear its ugly head again. Once in a lifetime was enough—he wasn't going through this again with the Chadways, not even as a bystander. It was starting to wreak havoc on his household, and fouling his own wife's mood. This was all Bird and Teri talked about.

Kenny paused. "That's not the point."

"It *is* the point. Only you know the answer to this, brother. And since you asked me, you better put all this into perspective—hold it up against thirteen years, and ask yourself if you're ready to walk on a mere case of flirtation. Pride goeth before a fall, man. Every time out."

Kenny drained his beer. "I've bought her flowers, and tried to be more attentive. I'm no Romeo, and shouldn't have to be for a basic level of respect."

"What kind of flowers did you buy?"

Kenny sighed hard. "I don't know—pink ones."

"Roses?"

"No. Carnations."

Lem shook his head.

"What kind of wine did you buy?"

"I don't know. It was on sale."

"No further questions, man." Lem shook his head again and slumped in the kitchen chair.

"But she's my wife!"

"Yup. After you being her first love, never experiencing what another guy could be like, and after thirteen years of cleaning your house, washing your drawers, standing behind you through thick and thin, giving you three beautiful children, and raising them like Mother Teresa, Maxine has been there." Lem couldn't believe he'd said it himself; Bird's argument had taken root in his mind. Damn, a married man didn't stand a chance. Wives had a way of drilling a concept into a man's skull like Chinese water torture!

Silence sat down at the table with both men.

"The woman has let a lot of stuff slide, Kenny. Had to, in thirteen with you," Lem said in a weary tone. Hell, he was out there now. Might as well go the full monty.

"Oh, so now you're on her side?"

"I'm on the side of your marriage not falling apart, 'cause I love both of y'all, man."

When Kenny didn't speak, Lem pressed on. "I guess

you never felt a little charge out of some good-looking sister giving you the eye, huh? Guess your battery is just dead. Never once crossed your mind when we rolled to the strip joint that time, and the ladies up there looked sorta good? Just a passing thought, but nothing you would act on. You know, the kinda thing that happens when you've been taken for granted lately—never happened to you?"

Kenny hung his head and looked at the floor.

Lem was amazed. So this was how the women always won an argument: they wore you down using history as the grinder.

"No, I didn't think you ever thought, 'What if'— but then came on home like you were supposed to when it got thick." Lem let his breath out hard, stood, and grabbed two more beers, sliding one across the smooth kitchen table for Kenny. "Just checking."

"All right. You've made your point. But I don't want her to go back to that class."

"You need to worry about what's happening at home, not out at some class. If things are so shaky that you have to be constantly looking over your shoulder, then it doesn't make a difference." Lem opened his arms wide. "This class, that class, the other movie, the mall—what are you gonna do, put Maxine under house arrest? That's no way to live, brother."

"It's not. I can't live like that."

"Okay, now you're being honest. So, what're you gonna do? Just throw in the towel?"

Kenny stared at his friend, who was making way too much sense. "Naw."

"Then go back in time. What is Maxine interested

in? What does *she* like? When was the last time you just went all out for *her?* Think about it. What does she do that you like?"

"Used to draw me a bath every Wednesday night when I came in beat up from the shop, and massage my back."

"You ever do that for her?"

Kenny shook his head and kept his gaze fixed to his bootlaces.

"You told me the house was a wreck. Why don't you go home and clean it while she's gone, man?"

He glanced at Lem from the side of his eye. "That won't make any difference at this point."

"Please. You are so out of touch. And have some roses sent to her damned class, to show that suave son of a bitch that you're confident enough to allow your wife to be in his presence, but she is still coming home to you. Kenny, man, where's your fight?"

"Send roses to the class . . . at night?"

"Give some kid an extra twenty to take 'em 'round there. Put a nice note on there, wishing her success. The next week, I'd send two dozen. After that, the last day, I'd be waiting outside with a bottle of champagne to congratulate her for doing so well, with hotel keys in my hand."

"That's crazy, *and* a waste of money."

"Mark your territory, brother."

Both men stared at each other for a moment.

"Thought I did that when I put a band on her finger," Kenny said stiffly.

"You did. But that marking is getting sorta old—scent is fading after thirteen years," Lem chuckled. "So re-mark it with authority, and then plant your flag—you hearing me?"

Kenny looked up at him and pounded Lem's fist.

"See, now we're getting somewhere. A man's gotta have a plan."

"I'll mark my goddamned territory, all right. Maxine's nobody's girlfriend—she's my wife."

"I hear you."

"That's right. No man is going to take her away!"

"Sho' you right, brother."

"I'll kick his natural ass."

"Uh-huh. I got your back."

"Touchin' my wife's hair, and what not."

"Disrespect, Kenny. The brother was dissin' your world."

"Not anymore."

"Fight for her."

"I plan to do that."

"I'd read her whole book, cover to cover, and put a one-liner in every card to let her know I did." Lem took another deep swig of his beer and leaned back in his chair.

"Think so, man?"

"Since when does being a husband mean you get to stop being romantic for thirteen-year stretches? Gotta give it some extra effort every once in a while—ask me how I know."

"It hasn't been *that* long since I've done stuff for Maxine, though."

Lem sighed. Kenny was a tough nut to crack. "Well, answer me this—how long has it been since she's been *receptive?*" Lem immediately held up his hands when

Kenny snarled. "No. Sorry. That's none of my business, and I don't want to know. Answer the question in your own mind."

"A while."

"Then I rest my case."

"I'm still stuck at the part about the man putting a silver goddess in your hair, Maxine!" Bird swooned on the sofa and fanned her face. "Kenny's in trouble."

"No kidding," Teri whispered as she stood and began pacing. "He said all that to you, in *that voice?* Oooooh, girl. What are you going to do?"

"She has to just take a cold shower and go home, Teri." Bird popped up from the couch and used her hands as she spoke. "Maxine, you can't even think about this again. It's too dangerous. That's the kind of man that will make a woman call the wrong name at the wrong time."

The threesome laughed, then Teri became serious. "Maxine, you have to shake this. You made the right decision, and just because Kenny went all Kenny on you again is no reason to doubt your instinct and good sense."

Bird was more dramatic. "Maxine, you cannot stay here overnight. Kenny might get the wrong idea." Her little sister was pulling her arms to make her sister stand, but Maxine wouldn't budge.

"You know Kenny comes from the dark ages, but he loves you, Max. He really does. His armor is a little rusty, but you can't compare him to that tall, fine, cut-up hunk of a black Prince Charming that just blew your mind—that's not fair. The man was almost about to cry, Maxine. His voice was all shaky, and that is *not* Kenny by a long shot."

"Kenny misses his meals being hot, his clothes being washed and his basic necessities taken care of. A good maid and nanny could replace me any day, just like take-out at a soul food joint could. But me, Maxine, the woman . . . somebody to cherish? Kenny can't miss that, because he doesn't know who I am." She wasn't sure why she was fixated on this, or why all the losses and years had come crashing down around her, but she wanted to scream, to yell, to cry, to make her sisters really know just how much the reality of losing her husband as a friend had wounded her. It seemed that nobody understood—least of all, Kenny.

"Call Lem," Teri ordered Bird. "Tell him to tell Kenny that this is serious. He's finally gone too far. He needs to make arrangements to get the kids to school in the mornings with their clothes washed and their lunches packed. Maxine isn't coming home for a while and needs a break from all of them."

Bird opened and closed her mouth.

"Thank you, Teri," Maxine sighed, curling up in a little ball on the sofa.

"Teri, have you lost your mind!"

"Bird. It's all right. It'll just be a day or so."

"But Teri. If they don't face each other, the situation could go from bad to worse!"

"Hand me the phone." Teri took the telephone from Maxine, who passed it to her with disinterest. She tapped her foot as she waited for the call to connect. "Lem, I need to talk to Kenny." Teri's head bobbed as she listened to Lem fill her in. "Well, then you call Kenny and explain that Maxine will be staying here for a few days. Right. I know, I know. Just let her have some space." Again Teri paused. "Well, then he'll have to make arrangements, since he doesn't appreciate a thing Maxine does. That's right. He can take them to school, and make lunches, and neither Bird nor I will help. We will not cook and clean for him. We *will* help with the children. And you tell him he needs to prepare a dish for Sunday, too—if he wants to eat with the family."

Teri pulled the telephone away from her ear. Bird covered her mouth, her eyes wide. Maxine sat up on the sofa as Lem's deep voice boomed into the receiver.

"That's our final offer. Take it or leave it. Kenny has to prove that he's serious about saving this marriage. Otherwise, there are other offers on the table that Ms. Joseph—also known as Mrs. Chadway—might have to consider. Tell your client that our client has options. Tall, fine, available, hankering, literary options that our client is really thinking hard about—that we're sitting on her to keep her from leaving the house to further investigate. Tell him, Lem. Good-bye."

Maxine was on her feet. Bird was whirling around in a frenetic silent scream. Teri stood with the dead phone in her hand, triumphant.

"Oh, my God, Teri. What did you do?" Maxine's voice caught in her throat.

"Oh shit, Teri!" Bird's voice came out in a high-pitched squeak.

Teri shrugged. "It was getting late; I have to be in court tomorrow. We needed closure. Maxine made it clear she wanted to play hardball, so I'm negotiating her terms—hardball style."

"What?"

"What!"

"Oh, don't worry, ladies," Teri scoffed, walking out of the room toward her bedroom. "We'll accept his counteroffer."

"Counteroffer?" Maxine was practically speechless.

"Teri has lost her mind."

"No, I haven't," Teri called over her shoulder before she turned to pace back toward them. "You wanted respect, equal consideration, and some measure of personal freedom within the workplace—namely your home. Right?"

"Yeah, but—"

"You wanted him to know that this time, you were serious. Right?"

"Yeah, but—"

"You wanted him to know what you were feeling, to experience a little of your angst, and to show some appreciation, correct?"

"Yeah, but this is crazy! Kenny's a good man. I love him. And, I don't want to hurt him. I just wanted him to hear me—"

Bird and Teri glanced at each other, then slapped each other five.

"Works every time for nuisance cases—hardball."

"I'll follow her home to make sure that's where she winds up. She's gonna be a little shaky for a few days. Needs to detox from the Gotier thing, but Maxine is strong—she's a Joseph woman."

Maxine gave each sister a soft punch on their arms and laughed. "Somebody call Lem back, so he'll call my husband, and we can get this all straight."

"She hasn't been out in a while," Bird sighed.

"I know," Teri agreed.

"*What?*" Maxine asked.

"Max is clueless," Bird sighed again. "The call has been made. You never retract a serious threat at the bargaining table. Just change your mind. Let sleeping dogs lie."

"Let him sweat for the next fifteen minutes while you drive home—then you go directly to bed and don't say a word. You are too tired for arguing and explaining. Plead the fifth. He's had an hour's lead time on you, according to Lem, and is over there probably bouncing off the wall. Serves him right."

"But—"

"You were wrong to be flirting with a man who would make the Pope jealous, but you just got a reprieve from having to hear about this for the next twenty years whenever you have a valid point to make—because Kenny will have to take the weight on this one. He jumped to a conclusion and was wrong. Now he'll have to take his lumps. And you get to get some deserved respect for your work, as well as for being a woman. Looks like you win big in the end."

"Bird, it was deeper than that, and about more than that," Maxine argued in a soft tone.

"Deeper than what?" Bird sucked her teeth as Maxine swallowed away a smile and glanced down. "Like our husbands wouldn't have that same shit-eating grin on their faces that you do if they got caught with J-Lo sweatin' them but came out unscathed, vows intact?"

"Makes a lot of sense when you put it all in context, Maxine." Teri chuckled and kissed her.

"He'll be so glad that you're home, he won't be trying to argue." Bird kissed her and then put her hands on her hips. "You might even get the house cleaned for once, if you act right, Max. And as for telling Lem—don't you tell my husband a thing. He can think that he narrowly escaped the wrath, too, and that might ensure he'll be on point for a few weeks himself. Whatever happens, Max, we're here for you."

"Oh . . ." Maxine gave her sisters a huge group hug.

ten

Per her sisters' express instructions, Maxine entered the house and went right upstairs. She'd noticed movement in the kitchen and knew it had to be Kenny, but she made a straight path to their room. She was so tired from the emotional roller coaster that she thought she might pass out.

Peeking out of the bedroom door, she rushed to the bathroom after she was sure the coast was clear. All she wanted to do was wash her face, brush her teeth, and crash. By rote, she turned on the spigot and splashed cool water on her face, lathered the facial cleanser in her palms, and swirled it on. She reached for the towel and buried her face in it, wiping away water and a new stream of hot tears with it. And then stopped.

Maxine sniffed the towel. It was a clean one. She stood up, dazed, and looked around the bathroom. Elves? Had to be. The bathroom was *clean?* "Nooo—"

Immediately her attention went to the toilet—the real test. She flipped the lid and inspected it. Sparkling porcelain winked at her. She closed the lid very slowly and stooped to survey the front of the bowl. White.

Gleaming white. Maxine pinched herself and stood slowly. Then her gaze tore around the room, and she snatched back the shower curtain and looked at the tile on the shower wall over the tub. Her finger went to the gout between the tiles and came away clean.

"Oh, my God . . ."

With trepidation, she exited the bathroom and went back to the bedroom. This time she fully took in the room. There were clean sheets on the bed. There were no men's socks and drawers on the floor. Was she in the right house? Her legs walked to the hamper. Empty. She tore out of the bedroom, down the hall to the kids' rooms, checking hampers in every one. Empty! She heard a vacuum cleaner go on down on the first floor. She trained her ears to another sound. The washing machine was engaged?

Although she wanted to go downstairs or reach for the telephone, she made herself go back to the bedroom. All the kids rooms clean? The *bathroom* clean? Kenny was running a vacuum cleaner. Good Lord!

The telephone jarred her, and Maxine reached for it without opening her eyes. A little disoriented, she yawned and glanced at the clock as she greeted the caller.

"Eight o'clock! I can't take a telemarketing call right now," she shrieked and hung up, flinging herself from the bed to race down the hall to wake the kids.

But when she barged into Ahmad's room, his bed was made, just as it had been the night before, and there was no sign of her son. Then it came back to her: the kids had spent the night at Bird and Lem's. But why didn't Bird call her so she could cart them to school? This was a mess!

Maxine raced to the bedroom and hit speed-dial. When the call connected, she didn't even wait for Bird to reply.

"You should have woken me up, Bird. The kids will be so late for—"

"Kenny got 'em," Bird chuckled. "Your attorney, Teri Joseph, was bargaining her behind off in your behalf last night. Remember?"

Stunned, Maxine sat slowly on the edge of the bed. "Yeah . . . but . . . but I didn't think he'd go for it. You should have seen how angry he was last night, Bird. He was so pissed, he probably cleaned the house to keep from killing me."

"Wrong." Bird giggled. "Only women clean when they want to commit murder. Guys just break up stuff and go get drunk."

"Well . . . maybe."

"We told you he loves you. You've got the day off. The baby is with Jay at Mrs. Jenkins's, and Kenny is taking off early to pick the kids up from school."

Alarm shot through Maxine as she clutched the receiver to her cheek. "You think my husband wants a divorce, after last night? He's getting self-sufficient, like he's trying to see if he can do this all by himself. . . . I don't like it, Bird."

Her sister laughed so hard in her ear that Maxine finally began to relax and chuckle with her.

"I sound crazy, right?"

"Duh-uh, Max."

Maxine laughed.

"Oh boy, have *you* been conditioned!"

"This change is a good thing, right?"

"Go have a slow cup of coffee this morning—*by yourself*, at home. You've got a rare day off with no husband *or* kids. Good-bye, crazy woman. I have to get to the salon. I love you."

"I love you, too, Bird. 'Bye."

For a moment Maxine stared at the telephone, and then hung it up. She took her time walking down the hall and going down the steps. She didn't know what she'd find down there. As she hit the bottom of the stairs, she gasped. A new world order greeted her.

There were no toys, the rug had been vacuumed, things had been straightened up, and there was no dust film on the television and stereo. She sniffed the air like a hunting dog. Lemon scent. The man had dusted?

She inspected each room as she walked through it toward the kitchen, and she stopped cold in the doorway as she glanced around it. The coffee was made, and the warmer light was still on. There was nary a dish in the sink . . . and the floor had been mopped. Oh, it was definitely the biblical end-of-days.

Trepidation threaded through her as she approached the coffeepot. She glanced at the kitchen table. He'd even moved her computer to wipe under it—she could tell. A small note was folded in front of the coffee with her name on it. Oh, God . . . she knew it. The Dear Jane letter. The I-want-a-divorce letter. Kenny was leaving her because she'd gone temporarily insane. Her hands shook as she lifted the small note and unfolded it. Maxine took a deep breath and willed strength. Her husband's scrawl was unmistakable. Tears filled her eyes.

Dear Maxine,

I love you and want my best friend back. Coffee is made, so have one at home. Enjoy your day off writing. See you for dinner tonight, but don't cook. I got that.

Love, Kenny

She covered her mouth with her fingers and closed her eyes, pressing the small note against her heart. He'd heard her.

Of course Shorty had called out again, Kenny grumbled, putting on his hat to respond to a tow job. *He* never took a day off, ever. Shorty was causing serious problems with his shop's schedule. Good thing Lem came in and opened up for him, but it irritated him no end that he had to take Shorty's runs—today of all days. Couldn't find good help these days—folks were so undependable.

Couldn't really depend on anything just going right. Kenny let his breath out hard. He was beat, and it was only ten o'clock in the morning. What had he been thinking about, staying up all hours cleaning a house? But Maxine was worth it. His wife did her job all the time without a break, without a day off. The realization gave him pause: nobody, especially him, had recognized that fact until it was almost too late. What if something had happened to Maxine? What if a tragedy struck and she were no longer around? What if she had never come home last night? She'd had to deal with that concept when he was in an accident; he'd never had to face that specter. Suddenly her words and resentment began to make sense.

A pang of guilt ran through him. He was glad that he'd retrieved her computer from the trashcan and wiped it off before she came home. That was uncalled for, just dumping it when he'd walked in the door, even though it had been one of the barriers between them. Kenny chuckled sadly to himself. Once he'd started wiping things off, he hadn't been able to stop and just kept going. Maxine was making him lose his mind.

But he wasn't about to lose her to anyone. Especially that Paul Gotier. For a crazy minute he thought about going to see Gotier and settling everything himself, the man's way. But it wouldn't win Maxine back or keep his kids if he did something stupid.

Kenny pulled his truck behind the stalled panel-body van on Martin Luther King Boulevard and jumped out. The March winds were easing up a little, thank God.

"What seems to be the problem?"

"Aw, this old girl just gave up the ghost," the elderly man said with a groan. He slapped the side of his van and shook his head. "Had her since I started my business, and even though the fellas say I should just trade her in, I can't part with her."

Kenny nodded, going around to the front of the van. "Pop the hood. Can you get her to turn over?"

"She's dead as a doornail. The fellas said I should have given her a tune-up more often, took better care of her . . . said I ran old Betsy into the ground."

Kenny let his breath out hard. "Yeah. The older they get, the better you gotta treat 'em. Need a little TLC, if you want 'em to go the distance. I can tow her wherever you like. You got a mechanic, or an auto-body place you want her to go to?"

The old man shook his head. "Just take her home. Jefferson's Florist." The old man rubbed his hands over his grizzled beard.

Kenny pulled a hook and chain behind him and then stooped. "All right. Let me hook her up."

"Damn, I just can't believe it! Have to get this whole load down to the McCormick Center for a convention, and she just up and quits."

Kenny peered into the back of the van and shook his head, and then remembered how much Maxine always liked flowers. Nice flowers. Exotic ones, not carnations. Fuchsia. That was her favorite color. That was the predominant color splashed throughout the van.

"Look," Kenny said, random thoughts slamming into his brain. "I hate to see another hardworking man in a bind. I could tow you to McCormick, and once you unload, pull you back to your flower shop."

"Aw'no, my man," his patron argued. "I don't have the kind of money to pay for that distance. It's gonna eat me alive just to get her to my shop."

"I'm the owner of my own shop, too, which means I can set the terms. I won't overcharge you—but I figure you have to get all these flowers to McCormick before they start to wilt."

"You're right. Could lose a contract, a load of flowers, and still have repairs to make on my van."

"Tell you what," Kenny said. "I'll take you down there on a barter."

"A barter?"

"Yeah. I need some flowers for my wife—nice, get-out-the-doghouse flowers."

The old man chuckled. "I understand, young fella.

Been there a time or two myself. But you must be a good man, 'cause most folks go the other way when they in trouble—be gittin' evil, nasty and whatnot, like it's everybody else in the world's fault. But I see you taking the weight for whatever ya did. I like that in a man."

Now Kenny chuckled. "Why would you assume that I did something wrong?"

The customer offered Kenny a jaunty grin as he appraised him. "You look stable, reliable—said you got your own business, which means you a thinkin' man. Don't seem the type to have a shaky wife."

"Naw, my Maxine is true blue," Kenny murmured, his gaze going off into the distance. He did have a good wife. God had definitely smiled on him when she'd come into his life.

The man snorted and extended his hand to Kenny, bringing back his attention. "You been married a long time, right?"

"Thirteen years," Kenny said with pride.

"Then by now, young buck—don't you know you're *always* gonna be the one who's wrong?"

Both men laughed and shook hands.

"Let's get you to the McCormick."

"And let's get you, good brother, out of the dog-house."

She was so nervous, her hands were shaking. Kenny had called and left a cryptic message about her children being at her sister's house again, and them needing to talk. At first she'd thought maybe he was waiting to sit her down and really let her have it. Not even her sisters seemed to have a clue about what was going on. Then a huge spray of flowers had come to the door . . . and heaven help her, Kenny had put a reference in there from their favorite song, Larry Graham's "One in a Million." Then, Kenny had called again and told her to get dressed up. Kenny never wanted to get dressed up. What was going on?

Maxine was the hardest person in the word to surprise. It had taken a veritable team effort. First Bird had to get her sister into the salon under a pretense, do her hair or something, sneak an all-clear call in to him so he could sneak home and get his gear, and then Bird had to shoo her out of the salon. Then Bird had to let him know Maxine was home, and Teri had to hold her on the phone long enough so the flowers could get there. But a part of him was warming to the idea of it all. He had to admit that, for the first time in ages, he was having fun. Even his son was in on the plan, helping to keep an eye on his mom. The best part of it all was, he'd come up with this crazy scheme all by himself. Huh—women weren't the only ones who could do espionage; Mata Hari could eat her hat!

As soon as she heard Kenny's keys in the door, Maxine was tempted to spring out of her vanity chair to rush downstairs. But something told her to just stay put. Whatever her husband had concocted, or wanted to discuss, she knew he had to take the lead on it this time.

On the telephone he'd complained that she was always the "cruise director." Maxine chuckled softly as she continued to apply her mascara. Didn't he know that she'd prayed for him to step in and handle some of the ongoing logistics around here?

But his weird behavior left a little tingle of anticipation in her belly. She hoped he'd still like her black dress. She hadn't worn it in so long for him. Maxine applied a dab of fragrance at her pulse points and stared at her reflection in the mirror, then dabbed a bit of perfume in her cleavage. Hopeful thought, she sighed. Most times, by the time they'd dressed up and ate, it was time to pick up the kids and come home—and they'd both be tired from just getting out for the night. How had they fallen into such a rut?

Footsteps coming up the stairs and then down the hall made her begin to rush. Then she reminded herself that Kenny still had to take a shower, get dressed, shave, and it might be a while before he was ready to go anywhere. Maxine slowed her pace.

But when his figure appeared in the doorway and she spied him in the mirror, she turned slowly to greet her transformed husband. Kenny looked good. . . .

"Hey, baby. Ready to roll?"

She had to force herself to speak. The man had on her favorite navy blue suit, with a powder blue button-down shirt, his best paisley tie, and collar bar. Maybe he was right, and her favorite color was blue. . . .

"In a minute," she murmured, still appraising him.

The way he was looking at her sent a current through her.

"You look really lovely tonight, Maxine." He glanced down at his shoes. "You hungry?"

Yeah, she thought, for you. Seeing him get all bashful released brand-new butterflies in her stomach. "You look very nice yourself, honey." She smiled. He must have turned himself inside out to surprise her like this. It really felt like they were going on a date.

"Epitome okay? You know, that restaurant down on South Michigan?"

"Epitome? We're going to *Epitome?*" Maxine set down her pressed powder and stared at the man.

"Unless, uh, you wanted something else? I can change the reservation, if you want."

"No, no, no. That's fine. That's really great. Wow—"

He watched his wife flush and turn toward the mirror again. She looked so pretty with her hair hanging down on her shoulders and held off her face by that little silver band. He could smell her perfume wafting toward him as he reveled in being able to lean on the doorjamb while she did her feminine thing. There was something about watching a woman primp and pout in the mirror for her man. And Maxine had a long, lithe spine that flexed as she leaned forward. She had gone all out and put on his favorite black dress. It showed off the nape of her neck just so, and clung just enough to reveal how her waist tapered into her slim hips. It also had a slit up one side that showed off her long legs.

Impatience tugged at him. He sure hoped he wasn't still in the doghouse tonight.

On the drive to the restaurant, music in the car had filled the conversational void. Her husband had thought of everything, making sure all their favorite CDs were within reach. He'd held her hand and told her to wait until he came around to open the door for her. Had he any idea what that did to her? After thirteen years, the man remembered to hold a door for her.

By the time they'd walked past the gorgeous marble columns and had been seated at a reserved table by the window, she didn't know whether to laugh or cry. There was so much she wanted to say to him, and every sentence began with an apology.

They laughed as they both tried to talk at once, bumping into each other's words after the maître d' had finally left.

"You first." He chuckled. "Ladies first."

"I don't even know where to begin," she said quietly, her eyes never leaving his face. "Thank you so much, Kenny. I love you, and I'm sorry. How did we get into that mess?"

"It doesn't matter how we got there—just so long as we don't stay there." He covered her hand with his. "I love you, too, baby. And I am so sorry that I ever took you for granted."

He gave her hand a gentle squeeze, which sent a warm, familiar current up her arm. They sat for what felt like a long time, saying nothing, just allowing their eyes to speak volumes. Thirteen years gave them that ability. Maxine closed her eyes briefly and sighed.

"I know," he whispered. "Feels good to be back to ourselves."

She nodded. "Oh, baby. You just don't know."

"Yeah, I do," he chuckled.

She laughed with him. "Yeah, I guess you do."

Kenny motioned for the waiter, and to her surprise, ordered champagne.

"Champagne?"

"Can't I order some champagne for my wife, just because?"

She smiled and glanced down. "Sure. I guess you can."

"It's a homecoming celebration." Kenny offered her a wry smile.

She laughed. "I'm busted, aren't I?"

"Totally." He laughed. "I'm not ashamed to admit that you had me worried."

He had no idea how flattered she was by that admission.

"You didn't have anything to worry about," she soothed, stroking his hand.

"Please. Maxine, I'm an honest man, and I had reason to worry."

She swallowed away a sly smile. "No." When she glanced up at Kenny, his expression was open and his eyes still seemed a bit haunted. She traced the back of his hand with her finger. "No . . . my husband has beautiful hands. Strong, from an honest day's work," she murmured. "He comes home so tired from doing all that he can to support me and the kids." She looked up at him fully now. "He's my first boyfriend. The only man I've known, and no one else comes close. My husband can speak to me just with a look. He and I, we go waaaay back. My mama and daddy gave him the a-okay."

"Maxine," he said slowly, looking down at their hands, "I also promised them, just like I promised you, that I'd love, honor, and cherish you all the days of our lives."

Her husband's words made her swallow tears, and his

handsome face was becoming blurry. He glanced up and held her gaze.

"I have always loved you and always honored you, Maxine Joseph Chadway—but I forgot how to cherish you over the years." Kenny let his breath out hard and shook his head. "Honest to God, Maxine, time and routine snuck up on me—and I got used to things always being a certain way. It wasn't until I sat down and read your book, remembered the little things we did together, and heard the pain on those pages about what it was like to not have the little random acts of kindness, as you called them, done for you anymore, baby . . ."

He put a finger to her lips when she tried to interrupt him. This time he needed her to hear and know, once and for all, everything she meant to him. "Our own son saw things falling apart, and he tried to tell me. Then I saw another man holding your hands like this . . ."

Kenny drew a breath to keep his voice steady, but there was no accusation in his tone. "And I knew that if Gotier saw in you what I did, a beautiful woman inside and out, and if he'd read all about how you were this vibrant, passionate woman who came from solid roots and good family, a good mother, like Mama Joe, who was being taken for granted—he'd do what any man in his right mind would do: scoop you up and never look back. I can't blame him for taking an open shot. Yeah, I was angry, but truthfully, I was more scared that my worst fear had come true, and I had only myself to blame."

Kenny sighed. "I knew I was your first and only.

And I was real lucky that I plucked you from the high school bouquet before you had a chance to really get out there and do some comparison shopping. And incredibly lucky that you loved me back."

"I have never comparison-shopped, because there is no comparison," she whispered.

"Maxine, you were and are still the prettiest flower in the bunch, and also the smartest. I've always asked myself why a woman so brilliant would have wasted her time with me." His gaze slid away from hers to study the table. "I always wondered when the day would come that you'd go off to college and maybe decide to—"

She shook her head and stopped his words. She saw the flicker of insecurity in Kenny's expression, and she never wanted him to have that in his soul again. She'd had no idea that he'd carried this silent worry all these years. Her foot slipped out of her shoe, and her stocking-covered toes crept up his calf until he smiled.

"My husband is fine, too. He doesn't need to work out in a fancy gym; his job is a workout—lifting cars and trucks like the Incredible Hulk. And he has his own business, which takes a lot of brains and courage to run. I already made my choice years ago, and I'm happy with my selection, thank you very much. Humph. I picked the best in the bunch, too."

Kenny laughed. His wife was such a nut. And she was a doll. But had she any idea what her words on those pages, and the words now coming from her gorgeous mouth, were doing to him? Or the way the lazy stroke of her hand upon his, with her toes running up and down his leg, was affecting him? She used to do that to him when they were dating—say things that made him feel ten feet tall, then touch some innocuous part of his body and drive him crazy, because he had to wait until there was an opportunity to explore more of her. He'd been a fool to ever doubt his Maxine . . . and even more insane to risk losing her by sheer neglect.

"I want my best friend back, Maxine."

She nodded. "I want my best friend back, too, Kenny." Her toes caressed the inside of his calf.

"You'd better cut it out, Maxine." He smiled.

"I'm not doing anything," she giggled, not even stopping when the server brought the champagne. "What am I doing?"

She lifted her champagne to Kenny in a silent toast, which he met, her toes and hand still stroking him. It was as though her touch was a healing balm. It soothed his battered pride, just watching her softly work on it.

"You know, we guys miss things, sometimes—that we shouldn't," he finally said. "But when they're gone, we feel it worse than y'all know . . . and sometimes we don't know how to put things into words . . . or listen, really. Men miss things."

"Miss things?" Maxine arched an eyebrow and tilted her head, not sure whether he meant overlooking things, or missing in their absence—but knowing exactly what he meant about not knowing how to put things into words. That had been her struggle, too. For a long time she didn't know how to define the problem, or what was bothering her, so how could she totally blame him for not hearing what was so hard for her to articulate? She patiently watched him try to find a way to describe what was going on inside his head.

"Like how you change the sheets every Wednesday before I come home," he said quietly after a moment, "and spray your perfume on them." He looked at her briefly and then glanced away. "I missed that; didn't realize how much I liked that until it was gone."

Understanding entered her as she began to decode his male language. Missed meant overlooked. Maxine gazed at her husband, her eyes gentle. "I didn't know you even noticed."

"Yeah. I do now. And like how you go to the trouble to make sure the bathroom is spotless that night, so I can take a bath. It doesn't get any plainer than reading about it in black and white. Maxine, I'm sorry . . . you shouldn't have had to write a manual for me to figure it out. Like I've always said, you're the one in the relationship with the brains."

She smiled.

"You do things for me, too, baby . . . things I don't always say to you, but that I dearly appreciate. Like I never have to worry about fixing anything around the house—you just do things that need to be done. And the way you are with the children . . . it's so nice to have a man who loves his family that way."

"And how you always put a little surprise in my lunch," he said. "Like I was going on a field trip every day."

She sipped her champagne and looked into the candlelight, feeling friendship, familiarity, and mutual appreciation rekindling within her.

"Or how you shoo the kids off to bed on those special nights, just so we can have some time alone."

Maxine nodded, her fingers now entwining his. He

had indeed heard her, and had read her actions for the tiny gestures of deep affection that they were.

"You put on that shea butter stuff, because you know I love the way it makes you smell, and you make something just beyond the doctor's orders for dinner, for me alone on that night. Every morning, you make my coffee and bring it up to me, then wake me up with a kiss before you have to scoot off to do a million other things. Sundays, even though you're rushing to church, you leave me a big plate of my favorite stuff."

He couldn't help it . . . and it was so crazy to even swear that he wouldn't do it again, but his hand left hers and his finger found that special spot down the side of her cheek. He watched her close her eyes, and his hand trembled. That's what had sent him into a rage. Someone else had dared to trace the side of her face, to put his finger near that special, special place that made his wife close her eyes. She caught his hand, opened his palm, and pressed her lips into the center of it to leave a burning mark. That's when he was sure. His spot was still his.

"I was foolish, Maxine. Got so spoiled by the things you do, I assumed they'd always be there. But when you stopped doing them, I missed them. I miss you . . . everything about you."

"I haven't gone anywhere," she murmured against his knuckles. "I started taking you for granted, too."

"Nah," he chuckled, withdrawing his hand and picking up a menu. He had to. If he kept touching his wife like that, they wouldn't make it through dinner.

"I never even worry about security. Kenny has it covered," she whispered. "If something in the house breaks, my husband will fix it. He can fix anything. If something goes bump in the night, my man will scare it away. If something sounds funny on the car, just leave it off at the garage. Trash? Kenny takes that out every Tuesday night. If my son misbehaves, he can wait till his father gets home."

The way she looked at him burned, and he glanced down at the menu, needing a break from her penetrating eyes. Maxine could always see past the macho and peer into his soul. For a long time, he'd been her hero, and she had no idea what it was like to begin to feel old, no longer her teacher, no longer the one showing her new and different things . . . or how useless he'd come to believe he was to her. But she was telling him that she still looked up to him after all these years, all the squabbles, tribulations . . . and her voice still held a touch of awe.

Maxine let her gaze rove over her husband, realizing just how close they'd both come to allowing it to all fall apart. Insecurities, routines, not understanding the other's need for attention and time. The admissions he'd just made to her had to be so hard for him, yet he'd opened himself up nonetheless. This is what they used to share: the friendship, the honesty, the willingness to compromise. In this moment, everything that had happened seemed moot. In this moment, she fully remembered why she'd fallen in love with this man. She remembered why she'd wanted to have children with him, and to share a life with him. Together they'd built more than a house; they had built a home. He was her best friend—though thick and thin.

Kenny looked up from his menu to his wife's gorgeous, tear-filled eyes. The candlelight seemed to dance in the extra liquid that rimmed her lashes, and she didn't even bother to blink back the emotion. It had a devastating effect on him.

"I love that man I depend on so much," she whispered, "and I have so much respect for him. He does so many things that I have also taken for granted every day. God forgive me that I ever made him wonder about my love or respect. He doesn't deserve that. He's my best friend."

A lump had claimed his throat as he stared at this woman, his wife, his best friend. He didn't know what to say, and could only convey the depth of his feelings with a gentle squeeze to her hand. Telepathy had been reestablished between them, and he watched her smile broaden as she picked up her menu. Yeah, she knew. This thing between them had grown as thick as a summer storm.

"You hungry?" She looked at him.

"Nothing on the menu grabs me."

She chuckled. "We came all this way and got all dressed up."

He nodded, but was beyond the point where he could laugh about anything.

"They have fantastic seafood here."

He just nodded. "Order whatever you think will be good."

She looked up immediately, her eyes wide. "Oh, my . . ."

"Yeah. It's that bad."

"Uh . . ."

"Been a while."

"I know."

"Order the food, Maxine." He sent his gaze out the window. Damn, it hadn't been this intense between them in a long time. But he had to think of something else. He had a whole itinerary planned. She deserved the total package.

"Okay," she finally whispered. But her gaze never left his face.

"You want some dessert?"

He studied his wife's expression and simply nodded.

She chuckled and shut the menu.

"Order it to go, baby," he said.

"You sure you want to wait that long?"

"I have to."

Maxine covered her mouth and laughed behind it. "Kenny, noooo . . ."

He chuckled. "I need a cup of coffee, and some *light* conversation, Maxine. Put your shoes back on . . . please."

She was seriously giggling now. "Want me to go get the coats?"

"Now, how would that look?"

"Better than—"

"You're crazy."

"I know . . . but I'm flattered."

He snorted, but was smiling. "It was that book of yours."

She stared at him. "You read it *all*?"

"Yeah. Okay, I read it all . . . if that was all right?"

"All right?" Her voice had practically purred the words.

"It took me back. I can't shake it out of my head."

If he hadn't consumed half a bottle of champagne, he'd swear that her eyelids had partially closed. She seemed to be sipping air through her mouth through barely parted lips. It was working his nerves down to a nub. Her mouth doing that, like that. He needed a cup of coffee and a mental diversion, *bad*.

"You liked it?"

Kenny hailed the waiter and ordered a cup of coffee, not able to answer his wife. "Maxine, you want something, baby?"

"Uh-huh," she drawled.

The way she said it had even made the waiter blush.

"Maxine, uhmmm . . . dessert—from the menu?"

"Oh, yes, uh, I need a moment."

He waited until the server left them again. "Want to go dancing? It's been a while since we've gone out stepping."

Was her husband insane? Dancing, now? After dinner took so long? And in public, the way she was feeling at the moment? He'd read her work and liked it! Kenneth Chadway had read her work and not just liked it, but *responded to it*, understood it, and was trying his best to change.

"No," she breathed. "Take me home. You read my work."

He hadn't marked his territory; he'd closed the borders and launched a nuclear response. His wife was melting down, and seeing her like that was not improving his odds for getting out of the restaurant without turning heads.

"But Maxine . . ."

"Please, Kenny. I really, really need you to take me home. You read my book. . . . Have you any idea?"

Aw, to hell with protocol. He couldn't take his eyes off her as he hailed their server. "Can you get a check back here, pronto? Something came up—uh, an emergency of sorts—and we have to leave."

The server nodded and just smiled.

Before he could close the driver's-side door, Maxine was practically in his seat with him. "Baby, I can't get us home like this," he mumbled as she repeatedly pressed her mouth to his.

"You read it. Kenny, you have no idea . . ."

"Baby, I can't see to drive." He chuckled.

She begrudgingly let him go, and he couldn't wipe the smile off his face. It had been a long time since he'd gotten that reaction. For a moment there, she gave him a high-school-make-out-in-the-car flashback. It was so simple, and he'd been foolish not to understand it before now. Maybe even plain old stubborn, set in his ways. If he had just listened to her sooner, really listened—or read her words—they could have avoided this whole mess. He would have known Paul Gotier was no threat, nor was Maxine's need to express herself. Kenny shook his head and chuckled quietly. Some people just had to learn everything the hard way.

"This isn't the way home," she said in a sexy, low tone.

"I know, baby. We'll get there . . . but I thought it might be nice to go dancing."

Disappointment etched across her face, making him drop his foot on the gas. If his wife wanted him as much as he wanted her, then he would not keep the lady waiting.

Maxine let out a sigh as he pulled up to the Bronzeville Bed and Breakfast. She didn't have a clue, and he had to steady his breathing as he casually spoke to her.

"You know, they have a small, intimate little club in here now."

"Really?"

He could tell that she'd tried to force her voice to sound upbeat, and her smile appeared strained.

"Yeah, I thought we could check it out. We have all night—no need to rush things."

Maxine just sighed and nodded, and waited for him to open her door. That old man he met today was something. A romantic from way back. That's why he became a florist, he'd said. Liked to see people in love. He was the one who'd told Kenny about this place, but the plan was Kenny's alone. Kenny fidgeted with the key in his pocket. Yeah, dancing was in order—but not on a dance floor.

He had to keep himself from chuckling as Maxine pleasantly waved at the front-desk clerk, and he absolutely loved the way she nestled against him as they walked. It felt like a real date.

"You have to have a key to get into this club?" She studied him hard as he opened the suite.

"Yup," was all he said as he flung open the door and stood back.

Maxine stepped across the threshold like a deer testing the asphalt of a highway. She put one foot over the line, looked around, and then moved forward with caution. Then she spun on him and filled his arms.

That was the reaction he'd been waiting for.

She could barely breathe, she was clinging to Kenny's lapels so hard. Fuchsia flowers were everywhere in the sumptuous suite, which looked like it had been appointed for a honeymoon. She was laughing and crying and kissing his rugged old face, and then she broke away from him to really take it all in.

"Let me have your coat," he murmured.

Walking over to the high four-poster bed, she ran her fingers over the handmade goose-down quilt. The lights went low behind her, and she heard music waft around her.

"May I have this dance?" Kenny extended his hand and she gave him her coat.

"With pleasure."

He tossed her coat onto an overstuffed chair and began a familiar slow dance in the middle of the floor. Larry Graham's love anthem enveloped them, just as Kenny's big, strong arms encircled her. Delirious with satisfaction, she fused to his body and breathed in deeply. God, her husband smelled so good, but not half as good as he felt. This was *their* song. This was their night. This was incomparable . . .

No one knew how to slide his work-roughened hand down her spine like that, or just where *the* spot was on her throat—or when it needed to be kissed. Years of harmony led that dance. The man in her arms had helped her find and claim all those spots he was working now. Nobody in the world could make her knees buckle like they were doing at the moment . . . and nobody but her Kenny could make her lose all shame and beg to be taken to bed.

* * *

"Where'd y'all go? To the Bahamas, or something?" Bird held the telephone receiver close to her face, glanced at Teri, who was hanging on her every word, and shrugged. "You *are* coming to Sunday dinner, right?"

"Ask her what time they'll be here." Teri was pacing and trying to tend a pot of greens at the same time.

"What?" Bird's eyes got wide, and she covered the phone with her hand. She glanced at Teri, and then Lem. "Our sister says that they didn't have time for her to cook. She was busy, so she's buying store-bought pies for dessert."

"My man!" Lem chuckled, as he left the room. "But tell him to come get his kids—now."

Bird held the telephone closer. "Maxine, have you lost your mind? Store-bought pies? Teri always brings the desserts from a bakery, not you. What happened to your macaroni and cheese you promised—the one you make every week?"

"What's she saying, Bird?" Teri walked in a circle now.

"They're laughing. I can hear Kenny in the background laughing."

"Girl," Bird fussed, "your children are asking for you all. Did you know your son doesn't go to bed on Saturday nights? He stays up late—and it's hard to, uh, relax with a teenager in the house—down the hall."

Teri shook her head.

"Maxine, have a heart," Bird pleaded. "Come home. It stormed on Friday night, and Kelly jumped in the bed with us that night. Are you hearing what I'm saying? Wednesday night, Thursday night, Friday night, and *Saturday* night? Not that I don't love my nieces and nephew, or anything, but . . . You *are* coming home tonight, right? Y'all haven't gotten into another blow-up argument, have you?"

"They're okay, right?" Teri was now wringing a dish towel between her hands. "They didn't call the entire weekend. That's not like Kenny and Maxine. Something could have happened, and gotten out of hand. Tell her we're worried. Seriously, Bird. We didn't even know where they were, in case of emergency—all we had were their cells and Kenny's pager number!"

"You hear that, Maxine? Teri and I were worried sick."

Bird looked at Teri for support. "They're laughing, Teri. Just laughing! Talking about running away from home for good and starting fresh. Oh, Max. I can't take another day. I'm used to only one little one—and he *sleeps.*"

"Laughing? We'll probably have another niece or nephew on the way." Teri leaned against the sink to hold herself up.

Bird began talking to the laughing couple on the telephone, and to Teri all in one breath. "Lem had to open the garage on Friday, 'cause Kenny called out sick—and he *never* in his life, except for a car accident, called out. I took the kids to school, and Lem picked them up. We were both so wiped out, I don't know how they did this for thirteen years. How did y'all *do* this?" Bird held the receiver so her mouth was directly in front of it. "Maxine Chadway, you and Kenny stop laughing this instant, and bring your butts over here right now!"

Maxine hung up the telephone and rolled over on her back, her laughter blending with Kenny's sonic booms of mirth.

"Maxine, I think next time we'd better check into a big hotel. I'm half scared to go down to the front desk and look people in the eyes."

She couldn't stop laughing as Kenny shook his head. "I'm sneaking out the back door, myself," she wheezed through the giggles. "You didn't even let the maid get in here to change the sheets, Kenneth Chadway. Three days, with food being shipped in from the outside? Look at this place. Old spare ribs, Chinese food cartons, fish platters—looks like the inside of a Dumpster in here. Total decadence." By habit, she started cleaning up.

"Maxine . . . stop."

They both looked at each other again and fell out laughing.

"Yeah, baby. I could do this once a month—even if just an overnighter. Damn, this was good."

"They've probably posted our pictures in the lobby to bar us from this joint, Kenny!"

"Yeah," he said, laughing harder, appearing totally triumphant. "The couple that acted ridiculous, and literally rocked the house." He rolled over and stroked her side as she neared the bed again.

They surveyed the room. Besides the scattered remnants of food, some furniture had been upended, and a picture that formerly hung on the wall was now perched on the seat of a chair.

He couldn't stop laughing as she dodged his grasp when he tried to pull her back into the bed. Maxine replaced the picture in its rightful spot. "That happened when you wanted to dance with me naked. Told ya not to get near the wall," Kenny chided.

She gave him a wink as she lifted her dress from the floor with two fingers. "Oh, these clothes are a mess. We'll have to sneak home and change."

"Why? All ya gotta do is smooth 'em out. We haven't had 'em on all weekend."

"I'm going home to put on something else."

"Baby, just take a bath with me, and we'll say we just came from church."

She stared at her husband. "You gonna tell a lie on the church? You need to stop. You are not serious? "

"I am very serious."

"But I gotta go to the store to pick up the pies."

"You're not cooking?"

"You want me to cook, or to take a bath with you?"

"You don't ever have to cook again in your life."

"I want that in writing." Maxine threw her head back and laughed again. "What time is it?"

"We've got about an hour, then we have to check out. How about if I pay for one more day, we leave at three-thirty, beg Teri to stay over at our house with the kids, and escape again? By now Lem's probably got a nervous twitch—he lost a Wednesday and a Saturday night in this transaction."

"This is getting to you good, isn't it?" She laid down and melted against him.

"It's always been good to me, baby." He found that special spot on her neck and nipped it. "I just got crazy for a while, and almost forgot."

"Is that why you were marking your territory so hard?"

He held her back and looked at her. "Uh . . . I wouldn't put it like that, Maxine." But when she laughed, he relaxed. How did women know things like that?

"Planted a flag in it, is what you did." She kissed him long and slow. "Loved every minute of it, too." Her eyebrow went up, and her expression made him laugh.

"You going to class next week?"

She nodded. "You worried anymore?"

"Nah . . ."

Ahmad wasn't at all surprised when his aunt Teri came into the room, stuttering—even though Aunt Teri always spoke in perfect speech. She was trying to explain where his parents were, and talking to him like he was a little kid. Ahmad sighed and smiled. It was cool. It was better for Aunt Teri this way, if he acted dense. Aunt Bird and Uncle Lem jumping in to try to explain just seemed to embarrass everybody worse, especially when Kelly asked a thousand questions and seemed like she was about to cry. One day his little sisters would understand, and one day the rest of the family wouldn't have to talk in code. He was just glad that his Mama Joe had heard his prayers to help Mom and Dad work things out, through thick and thin.

epilogue

One Year Later ...

maxine heard the voice filter into the kitchen as she broke snap peas. Just as clear as a bell, the voice came from the television that had been left on for background noise. One word pulled her from her task and made her go into the living room. *Hetheru.*

It seemed like a hundred years ago, when all of that happened. Maxine shook her head in awe. Time was a funny thing. Her belly didn't flip-flop for him anymore.

Paul Gotier sat on the set of a talk show, his legs crossed, looking fine and elegant, and his exotic tone drifted into her memory bank as he explained the premise of his latest book.

"This book came to me hard and fast; it was inspired work, if one looks at art from a spiritual level. Men love deeply, and get swept away. I wanted to reach down within my gut to explore this aspect of being the other man, and passed over for an honorable husband. Today's literature usually centers on that paradigm from the female perspective."

Gotier paused, took a sip of water, and let out a slow

breath as though composing the rest of his response. Perhaps he was composing himself, Maxine thought, her hand going to the lock that had held a silver goddess for a brief lapse of propriety.

"Hetheru is about an extraordinary woman, because she is so grounded, and her world is so authentic in its mundane capacity that she ironically becomes the protagonist's goddess, of sorts. His true acceptance of her decision doesn't come until she returns to his class, after they have revealed themselves to each other, and her husband sends her a single white rose—invading what had been the protagonist's and her sacred, private space until then."

"So is this Hetheru a real woman, or a mythical creature?" the show host boomed happily. "This book has stirred quite a lot of discussion, as it straddles the fence of being a love story and paranormal fiction."

"I leave that decision for the reader. But as in all mythology, a goddess cannot be possessed by a mortal man, who can only dream of her and admire her from afar. And like a goddess, she ultimately gives the character absolution, freedom—which is her eternal gift."

"But this gift is complex, Paul. They both learn from each other, right? Though not before she nearly becomes an obsession for him. There are a lot of psychological undercurrents, unseen drama happening in the characters' heads—which makes this book difficult to put down, but also hard for the reader to separate the mental action from actual physical events that are taking place."

"Yes. I have made some of the elements of this story intentionally vague, so the reader can decide what actually transpired. This man is trapped for a period by his obsession. Afterward, anointed by Hetheru's tenderness, he is able to go on. He can stop punishing himself and stop grieving for his failed marriage, because Hetheru cared enough to be a friend instead of a lover, and in so doing, she releases him. He teaches her the power of her voice, she teaches him the power of acceptance and forgiveness. He frees her voice, just as she frees his heart— but her voice must hold a secret about how close she came to straying, and his heart must get broken. Thus, the paradox."

The show host's next question didn't even register in Maxine's brain as she looked at the man who had briefly become her friend, and clicked off the television. She had heard him say he was deeply affected a year ago, but didn't fully believe it. And she had seen something indefinable flicker in Paul's eyes when an elderly florist brought her a single rose from Kenny. It seemed like a strange gesture, but now she truly understood that men marked their territory. Trying to put a tiny silver Hetheru in her locks had been Paul's attempt to send a signal to the incumbent male. Just as the rose was a warning shot from her husband.

Maxine made her way back to the kitchen, a little dazed, a little flattered, a little nervous. She had almost turned her whole universe upside down for a temporary issue playing itself out at home. A year gave things perspective. A rough spot in a marriage had to be measured over time with all the good, the ups and downs in context. What if she and Kenny had stopped there and thrown it all away? Pure relief swept through her. Good thing Teri had taken that business card, and was sensible enough to keep it in her office vault. Her sister was wise, and she was the one who sent out her manuscript, and who brought her into contact with her new agent. Everything went to and from Teri's office, to ensure all was aboveboard. And Bird had been a gem, too, acting like an electrified fence to protect her from temptation—even when there wasn't any need to, anymore.

Maxine had to chuckle. She was blessed. She had a wonderful family. Kenny was. . . . There were no words for how much she loved him.

And she was glad she had been able to tell Paul the things she did, on that last day of class. It was mother wit, learned the hard way; nothing special, she'd thought. Obviously she had been wrong. He was a friend, but one she couldn't keep. Because to have his friendship, given all that had happened, would violate the best friendship she had of all. Immortalized as a goddess? Hmmph, hmmph, hmmph.

Some truths were good to pass on through writing; some things were better passed on in the oral tradition of her people—told in a quiet voice in the kitchen, mother to daughter, father to son, maybe sister to sister.

Maybe.

Maxine began snapping her beans again, satisfied that her house was tidy. The baby would wake up from her nap soon, and then her kids and husband would be home.

Yeah. This one would go to her grave as an old lady's far-off smile.

**Visit the Simon & Schuster
romance Web site:**

www.SimonSaysLove.com

**and sign up for our
romance e-mail updates!**

Keep up on the latest
new romance releases,
author appearances, news, chats,
special offers, and more!
We'll deliver the information
right to your inbox—if it's new,
you'll know about it.

POCKET BOOKS

2800.02